THE ORDER
OF THE REDEEMED

WARREN CAIN

The Order of the Redeemed

Warren Cain

Print ISBN: 978-1-54396-702-9

eBook ISBN: 978-1-54396-703-6

PROLOGUE

Heat waves appeared in the distance across the fields outside the town of Jericho as Thomas made his way to the moderate-sized home he and Zacchaeus had been working on for nearly a month now. Thomas was surprised to see Zacchaeus already putting mud into the brick forms to be used for the home.

"How long have you been here?" the large man asked, realizing Zacchaeus must have been well into his second hour of work by the amount of bricks he had already formed.

"I can't wait on you all day, Thomas. We may never get all the work done if we started as late as you," replied Zacchaeus as he stretched his small but muscular-framed body to relieve the soreness he was feeling from several days of forming the mud bricks. His blue eyes seemed to glow as he welcomed his friend.

"Some of us don't have a wife that requires the kind of money I put out for your wages."

"I think it would be fairer to say that some of us are unable to attract such a woman who would be willing to marry us, and I don't want to hear how you can't afford a woman because you pay me too much when the truth is I make you money. How was your evening, Thomas?" he asked, turning the conversation from the usual morning ritual of seeing who could win in a verbal combat.

"Not too bad. I visited my mother last night."

"Didn't want to cook?"

Thomas smiled. "How late did you work last night? We didn't have near this much done."

"Until dark. I could use the extra money."

"Extra money is one thing. You didn't have time for a decent night's sleep. What do you want to work so many hours for?"

"We want to build a bigger house. We want to build one from stone," mumbled Zacchaeus, slightly slumping his shoulders.

Thomas breathed in through his nostrils as though he were a dragon, preparing his next breath to expel fire. "You mean SHE wants to. Do you know how much a stone house will cost you? By the time you pay the stone masons you could have built three mud brick houses yourself," scolded Thomas.

Zacchaeus stood with his head held down, his previously glowing eyes dimmed by the truth Thomas had spoken.

"I don't mean to sound hateful, but I just can't stand to see you treated so poorly. You're my friend, Zacchaeus. Does she try this hard to make you happy? You spend every waking moment working, trying to make enough to satisfy her endless wants."

Zacchaeus hesitated for a second as he fought back the urge to vocally agree with Thomas. He straightened up, trying to look as though he wasn't tired from the long days he had spent working to make enough money to keep Ezra satisfied.

"Me and Ezra have a good relationship," he lied.

The words didn't sound convincing, and he knew it.

Thomas only pursed his lips.

"We need to get back to work. There's a day's worth of bricks that are solid enough to be laid," Zacchaeus murmured, turning his back to Thomas.

I didn't mean to upset you, thought Thomas, *but you deserve better than this.*

*   *   *

The walk home from work through the dimly lit street gave Zacchaeus time to contemplate the long days he had been working and the amount of truth he had heard in Thomas's words. *He just doesn't understand that it would be nice to have a good house. He's never had more than a small house his whole life.*

He shook his head as he realized the argument was only to convince himself, and he wasn't believing a word of it. *I've never had a decent house. Probably because I don't make enough money to buy one, but how do I convince Ezra of that?*

The thought occurred to him as his current house came into view. He hesitated to admire the one-room home sitting on a growing mound created by the mud brick houses that had previously collapsed on which their house had been replaced.

I knew this house wouldn't last forever. It was already fifteen years old. Hard to get much more than thirty out of mud brick. With my skills I could build her a home from mud brick that would be as large as any home in Jericho.

Zacchaeus looked at the large cedar door they had purchased to be used on the new house when it was built. He thought of the table and chairs in the middle of the room that were built for a much bigger home and took up any living space they had.

Everything's too big for our little house. Every time she buys something it's so we can have it in our new house but it doesn't fit the one we have and it doesn't fit any that we can afford.

Zacchaeus opened the door to find Ezra sitting at the large table with a man Zacchaeus knew well as James, the regional tax collector for the Jericho area.

"Did I fail to pay you enough taxes?" asked Zacchaeus sarcastically.

Ezra stood.

"Zacchaeus," she scolded. Her dark eyes glared from underneath her harshly wrinkled brow. "I've asked James to come here to discuss you working under him as a tax collector."

Zacchaeus looked uneasily at James. The thought of being a tax collector caused him to shiver and he was sure the other two in the room caught the movement.

James stood.

"I'm going to put a bid in on the region to the east. I have word that with the offer I plan to make I should be placed in charge of that region also. I need some tax collectors to work for me. I'm short the way it is, and if I get the east region I'm going to need someone who lives in Jericho to look after it when I'm not in the area. Ezra tells me you would be good for the job."

When Zacchaeus failed to respond, or even move, James continued.

"It pays three times what you're making now and a little more if you charge extra."

James and Ezra shared a look that, along with the comment, caused them to laugh almost uncontrollably as though they were both in on some joke. Zacchaeus stood looking at them, not sure if the joke was about charging extra or if it was about his wages.

Neither one seems funny.

"I need some time to think about it," muttered Zacchaeus, tired from a long week of hard work and lacking the willpower to argue at the moment about his employment as a tax collector.

"I'm going to need an answer by next week," said James as he showed himself to the door. "It means a lot more money."

The door closed as the well-dressed James exited the house.

Zacchaeus sat down at the table, placing his arms in a folded position on the table and slumping his shoulders.

"What's wrong with you?" Ezra shouted with irritation as she slowly moved towards him as though she were a lioness about to attack her prey.

The tone caused Zacchaeus to slide down in his chair as if it would protect him from the oncoming assault.

"You're never going to make enough money to build us a house we can be proud of. Do you want to work as a stupid house builder your whole life? STUPID. That's what building houses is."

Zacchaeus stood abruptly. "IT'S NOT STUPID. I like what I do. We could afford it if we didn't have to build it out of stone." His voice rose. "I could build you a large house out of mud brick, one of the largest in Jericho. I have the skill for it. I'm sure Thomas would help me."

Ezra backed up from the harshness in his tone. In all the years they had been married, she had always been able to force him to do what she wanted with intimidation. "I'm sorry, Zacchaeus," she whispered, realizing she wasn't going to intimidate him into what she perceived to be a more appropriate job for HER husband. "I didn't mean to say what you did was stupid. It's just that you work so hard and you deserve to make more."

She put her hand gently on his shoulder and moved towards him until she was rubbing against him.

"Wouldn't it be nice to make more money so we can have a nicer house? Don't you want to take the tax collector job? For us?" She forced the frown from her forehead and replaced it with what she hoped would pass as a look that indicated she was feeling attracted to him. The feelings he held for her swept over him from the long overdue attention she was now showing him.

"I'll think about."

*   *   *

Zacchaeus made his way through the dusty streets towards the road that led from Jericho to Jerusalem.

"Looks like a good day," remarked Zacchaeus to the two Roman soldiers assigned to ensure the Roman taxation powers given to Zacchaeus remained intact. The well-disciplined pair gave no indication to Zacchaeus's comment as they kept perfect step with each other, as though they operated as one unit.

Zacchaeus shook his head slightly, failing to understand why the soldiers would not acknowledge any of his attempts at conversation. The trio made their way to the gateway on the edge of town, which marked the road that led to the marketplace.

"Sounds like the crowds are unruly today."

The guards made no comment concerning the clearly louder than normal crowd.

Zacchaeus allowed the soldiers to move in front of him. The above-average height, long spear, and sheathed sword combined with the confidence of the well-trained pair caused the crowd to step out of the way towards the buildings, allowing the soldiers and Zacchaeus the luxury of walking down the center of the street without the inconvenience of pushing through the large crowd.

"The numbers are right. Your toll adds up to six pieces."

Zacchaeus knew the voice belonged to Simeon, his newest and most promising apprentice.

Zacchaeus was amazed he took so well to overcharging. It had taken him two years before the pressure from Ezra and the other tax collectors allowed him to take more taxes from people than the specified amount. *I might as well*, he justified to himself. *They accuse me of it anyway.*

The first few times caused him lost nights of sleep, but gradually the overtaxing became easier and necessary to pay for the extra luxuries he became accustomed to. "You're wrong about the numbers—my brother passed through here two days ago with the same amount of stock and was only charged four pieces," exclaimed the man.

"What seems to be the trouble, Simeon?" asked Zacchaeus, assessing that the muscular man trying to pass through the gate had an advantage by knowing the tax amount from only two days ago.

"This man doesn't wish to pay his tax. He's accusing me of overtaxing him."

Zacchaeus walked to the gate. The man stood a head taller than him, and his dark tan and muscular build would have been intimidating were it not for the two soldiers flanking Zacchaeus.

"What's your name?" questioned Zacchaeus in a calm voice.

Anger was replaced with an inquisitive look as the question had its desired effect.

"Jerod."

"What seems to be the problem, Jerod?"

A wave of relief passed over Simeon's face as the more experienced tax collector diffused the out-of-control situation.

"My brother passed through here two days ago and was charged four pieces for the same amount of stock. Now I'm being told I must pay six pieces."

"That's right," expressed Zacchaeus with no hesitation. "The extra tax is new. It's a tax for new wells in the region."

Simeon was impressed at how smoothly Zacchaeus made up an answer that sounded so believable. The crowd, who only seconds before Zacchaeus showed up were ready to force their way through the gate, now, within the few short seconds to ponder the decision, the explanation from Zacchaeus, and the presence of the two soldiers, stood quietly behind Jerod. The mood shifted as the people looked to their leader, waiting for his next move. They had stood ready to defy the injustice, feeling as though they were about to protest for all the times they had been overtaxed. Now, with the arrival of Zacchaeus and his authoritative certainty, it seemed their leader, Jerod, would offer little or no resistance.

Zacchaeus remained quiet, understanding from the look on Jerod's face that he only needed a few more seconds to think about the situation before he would decide it wasn't worth the trouble and pay the six pieces.

"Pay the six pieces," demanded Simeon, stepping up to the gate with a look of arrogance as he now felt the argument he was losing only a minute before had turned in his favor.

No, thought Zacchaeus as he closed his eyes, certain that such a haughty demand would put Jerod on the defensive.

"How can you be so dishonest?" The words spilled from Jerod's mouth like venom from a cobra. The hate in his voice stirred the crowd back to the mob twitchiness Zacchaeus had just calmed them from.

The crowd waited for Zacchaeus to make his move. He had been called dishonest in front of them, and Zacchaeus knew his next move would either diffuse the crowd or cause them to riot.

There's only one choice.

Zacchaeus made eye contact with the soldier in charge. It was one of the few times since the soldier had been with him that Zacchaeus could remember him making eye contact. The soldier knew he would be needed to take care of this crowd. It was his chance to enforce Rome's ultimate authority, and he was ready to jump at this opportunity he considered an honor. A nod from Zacchaeus, and the two soldiers stepped forward and grabbed Jerod, allowing him no room for retaliation.

"No!" shouted Jerod, suddenly losing the courage he held only minutes before. "I'll pay."

The crowd stood quiet and afraid as they watched Jerod being beaten by the two soldiers.

* * *

Zacchaeus stopped halfway up the small road that took him around Jericho and to the backside of his home to avoid the shepherds that would be making their way to the well. He stopped to admire his recently built stone house that was by far the finest home in Jericho.

Ahhh. Good to be home, and what a fine home you are. A sense of pride overtook him as he viewed the large structure. His trip to Jerusalem had lasted only three days instead of the expected four, but he was glad to make it home to sleep in his own bed.

Zacchaeus opened the back door quietly and tiptoed into the house, hoping to surprise Ezra at his early arrival. A smile crossed his face as he noticed the large wooden table that now had a house more appropriate for its size. He tiptoed down the hallway towards the bedroom in an almost childlike manner.

His heart stopped for an instant as he approached the entrance to their stately bedroom. She lay in bed, her eyes closed with a look of ecstasy on her face. If her eyes had been opened, she would have seen him come into the room. He had never seen her face look so happy as her world of lies she had built around him crashed down. The man who was lying on top of his wife seemed oblivious to his presence. The thought of all he had done to try to make her happy, leaving his job with Thomas, becoming a tax collector, building this house for her. That was the betrayal. He worked so hard to make her happy—to remove that scowl on her face every time he was near her. Now, when she was unaware of his presence, the scowl was no longer there.

It's me that she despises. The thought seemed to come from somewhere deep in his mind as though it had always been there—it only needed to come to the surface and be put to words.

Ezra opened her eyes, and her expression changed to a look of horror.

"No!" She pushed the man off of her.

James, thought Zacchaeus as he recognized his boss.

Zacchaeus turned and walked down the hallway, unable to put anything he was feeling into words. As he sat down at the table he could hear whispered murmurs coming from the bedroom.

Zacchaeus grabbed his walking stick and clutched it with a tight grip, glaring into the hallway as a vision of beating James played through his mind. A feeling of defeat overtook him, and he swallowed the anger. *Why? After all I've done for her.*

The thought fueled the feeling of anger once again. *I don't have to beat him myself. I'll let the people outside do it for me.*

Zacchaeus stepped towards the door with a look of determination.

"Zacchaeus." The voice was soft and low as though she were gently trying to wake a child.

Zacchaeus hesitated. Tears ran down his face as the mixed feelings of defeat and anger tugged him in each direction. He turned, unable to utter any of the words inside him.

"I'm sorry, Zacchaeus."

She came to him and tried to put her arms around him. He pushed her back with a look of disgust.

"Why, Ezra? Why did you do this?"

"I needed more. You were never there for me."

"Never there. My whole life was built around what YOU wanted."

"You could have done more for me. If it hadn't been for me pushing, you would never have amounted to anything," she scowled.

The look of disgust toward him allowed the anger he was battling to rise again and overtake him.

"How dare you say that? I was happy. A lot happier before I became a tax collector. I despise it. But I did it because it was what you wanted. You wanted your big house and your fancy things, and this is how you repay me?"

Zacchaeus turned and walked towards the door.

"Please don't tell them." She grabbed his arm. "We can work this out."

He pulled his arm from her as though he had been touched by a hot piece of metal.

"Get away from me, ADULTERESS."

Zacchaeus turned and opened the door.

"No, please," she pleaded.

"ADULTERESS!" Zacchaeus shouted into the busy street. "ADULTERESS!"

The word made its way through the dusty street like a strong wind, impacting everyone in its path. The people exchanged uncomfortable glances. Several of the adults sent their children running home, almost certain this was about to turn into a horrible scene.

"Who? Who is the adulteress?" asked a gray-haired man with bushy eyebrows and green eyes.

"Ezra. My wife. I caught her with James the tax collector. They're inside."

Zacchaeus walked in through the door followed by several of the people in the growing mob outside. The back door was open, and James could be seen running away, already a good distance from the home. Ezra, who was now sitting at the table, arms in front of her with her head bowed, looked up with a blank stare.

"What do you have to say for yourself, woman?" quizzed the old man.

She shook her head, indicating she had nothing to say, then lowered her eyes, looking at the ground once again.

"Take her out of here," the old man shouted to the men who had followed him into the house.

"No! Please, no."

Her words had the effect of a cup of water thrown on a blazing fire as several men forced her towards the door. Her eyes made contact with Zacchaeus as she searched his face for any indication that he might help her. He shifted his eyes to the ground to avoid her stare.

The door closed, and Zacchaeus stood in the large quiet house alone. Outside he could hear the mob receding to the outside of town where he was certain Ezra would be stoned.

She had it coming.

We could have worked it out. Her words came back to him.

NO. No, we couldn't have worked it out.

He walked back to the bedroom as if to remind himself of why she was being taken away.

Our bed.

He came back to the room to remind himself of what he had seen only a little while before. Instead, he was overtaken by the feelings he held for Ezra as he thought of all they had done together. The whole house belonged to both of them. He felt he had also betrayed her by not giving them a chance, by having the mob take her away.

"EZRA!" he shouted, running out the door.

His heart raced as he followed the direction he heard the crowd take her. Zacchaeus ran down the street and up the steep hill. He struggled to push his way through the mob surrounding her. Between the frantically moving people in the crowd he saw several large stones strike the arms she held in front of her, protecting her head from the oncoming stones.

"STOP!" he shouted as he tried to push his way through the unyielding crowd. "STOP!"

Ezra entered his field of vision again. Her arms had now dropped. He could see her struggling, trying to keep them up. Zacchaeus was knocked to the ground by the jostling of the onlookers. He struggled to stand again.

"EZRA!" he shouted.

Her arms slowly dropped as the last bit of willpower gave in to the unrelenting onslaught of stones. Her eyes made contact with his as a stone echoed a hollow thud from the side of her head, causing her to effortlessly slump to the ground. Zacchaeus pushed through the crowd fueled by a sudden burst of rage.

"No!"

He placed his body on top of hers, holding his hand to the crowd.

"STOP!" he shouted.

A stone that had been hurled before he was there struck the side of his head, causing a bloody spray.

"Stop!"

He refused to move, not caring if there would be more stones. The physical trauma of the stones failed to match the emotional onslaught he was enduring. He held her limp body close, protecting her from the stones he was sure were coming.

The stone that caused the now dripping wound in the side of his head proved to be the last.

He turned to stare at the crowd. Several of them still held stones poised to throw. An eternity passed by as he waited for the crowd to decide how this scene would end. He had made his move to protect her and could only wait for their response.

A young, slender-looking man who earlier had shouted for her stoning in a rage of bloodlust made eye contact with Zacchaeus. The reality of the situation hit the young man as he saw the anguished look in his eyes. He dropped his stone and pushed his way out of the crowd. Slowly the rest of the mob followed suit and left.

Zacchaeus pulled away from Ezra, looking into her face for any sign of life. Blood and dirt had matted her long black hair. A large spot of blood from where the final rock had struck her caked the side of her face, down her neck, and into her clothes.

"It doesn't feel good to be cheated? Does it?"

Zacchaeus glanced up and squinted through the sun, trying to identify the only person other than himself who remained. The man stepped to the side to block the sun, allowing Zacchaeus to identify him.

Zacchaeus was speechless at the bruised face he recognized as Jarod, the man from the week prior whom he had beaten for calling him a cheater when he had overcharged him. A look of satisfaction crossed the man's deeply bruised face and red eye. He turned away, leaving Zacchaeus alone with her body.

A wave of guilt passed over him as he looked into her face that no longer scowled back at him.

"I'm sorry, Ezra," he cried as he pulled her close to him.

*　*　*

A large crowd began to pour into Jericho. Children ran through the streets shouting, and adults pushed to move in closer to the center of the crowd. Zacchaeus tried to get a closer look as well at the man who was causing all the excitement, but due to the large crowd this proved impossible.

He could not contain his excitement as he thought back to the way the woman had explained this man. "Jesus, he's a Nazarene. He's like no one I've ever seen before," she revealed. Her eyes lit up as she thought back to the day she met him. "A large crowd was preparing to stone me for adultery. He saved me." Her eyes glowed as she talked about Jesus.

Redemption from my sins, Zacchaeus thought to himself in amazement at the power this one man must have. It sounded so unbelievable, but in his heart, he wanted it so badly. He was to meet with him later today to discuss the circumstances of his redemption.

I don't think I'm going to be close enough to see him, and I know I won't see over these people, thought Zacchaeus as the crowd began to work their way to the center of town, pushing Zacchaeus back. He looked around and spotted a tree in the direction the crowd seemed to be heading. The gamble paid off. The mass of people swarmed around the tree as it came by.

Zacchaeus stared in amazement at the size of the crowd. He had lived in Jericho all his life and had never seen the city so full of people. He trembled at the thought that someone who caused so much interest would wish to see him. Zacchaeus spotted a man looking up in the tree and walking towards him. His gaze seemed to penetrate into his soul as if to say, "Time to rest from your guilt."

He wanted it so badly. To live free of the suffering, to sleep at night without waking, to once again understand joy.

"Come down, Zacchaeus, I must stay in your house," declared Jesus.

Zacchaeus jumped the twelve feet to the ground in his excitement. The crowd looked on spitefully for many of them knew Zacchaeus for the sinner he had been and were unwilling to let him change. As they entered the house, Zacchaeus could not contain his excitement. He offered Jesus a seat at the large wooden table that held two lit candles near the center.

"Margaret!" shouted Zacchaeus toward the rear of the house.

A young servant woman appeared from a back room.

"Margaret, bring us something to drink and prepare supper. We have a guest."

"What do you wish of me, Lord?" asked Zacchaeus, focusing his full attention back to Jesus.

"Only that you take the steps required to redeem yourself. Entire lives have been wasted on guilt, souls that were destroyed focusing on one mistake. I came to free the penitent from that guilt, that they may know joy again, to once again give them passion for life. You are the one that has been chosen to be the foundation of the organization which will provide many sinners with this opportunity. You have a choice, Zacchaeus. Do you wish to redeem yourself by working for a cause much greater than yourself?"

There was no question in his heart. The desire for redemption was with him all the time.

"What must I do?" he responded.

"Soon one of my disciples will deliver a cup to you. You will know it is my disciple when he says, 'The master is gone. This cup was used the last time I ate with my lord. He wishes for you to have it.' You will drink from that cup, and you will understand all the work you need to complete to begin your redemption."

CHAPTER 1

Twelve-year-old Kirk Murphy stood in the back of the Catholic church in rural Lansing, Missouri.

"Hello," he whispered in a quivering voice.

He looked down at his right hand, surprised to see a sword in it. He held the sword up in the dim light to admire it.

Wow. It's so shiny . . . and heavy.

He swung it from left to right and pushed it forward as though he were running it point first into something. He had played with cardboard swords before, but this one was real. A little heavier than he imagined it would be, but he felt he could manage it.

The church seemed so quiet with no one else inside. He looked at the front. The light coming through the stained glass windows softly illuminated the lower portion of the statues behind the altar. This gave Kirk a feeling comparable to someone who thought he may have just discovered a body part but wouldn't know for certain until he moved in for a closer look.

The pews slightly reflected the light off their varnished surface.

Kirk tried listening for any sound. He had never been in a place this quiet. It gave his ears a strange sensation to strain for the slightest background noise when there was none to be heard.

Be brave, he thought to himself, trying to stand taller.

The back of the church was decorated with statues. In the dim light, they seemed haunting. His imagination was giving life to the statues. He would look intently at them, focusing until he was certain their eyes moved. A chill ran down his neck.

In the back of the church he saw a statue of Michael the Archangel defeating the dragon. The statue stood about six feet tall, and the dragon was curled around the angel's feet with Michael holding a spear above him ready to strike his head; the dragon poised as though he would strike the angel's legs.

As Kirk looked at the statue he remembered being taught in Sunday school that the dragon was symbolic of Satan defeated by Michael and the angels in a war fought in heaven. The dragon's eyes moved. A chill passed through him. Kirk blinked and looked at the statue, waiting for the eyes to move again.

Must be my imagination.

The candles in the windows gave an eerie glow against the stained glass. Kirk moved behind the pews to the confessional, a small room about five feet by eight feet located in the back of the church.

From the dim glow of a streetlight through the stained-glass window adjacent to the confessional, he could see the door was slightly cracked open. Kirk thought his heart was going to pound out of his chest as he reached for the doorknob. Much to his own surprise, no thought of walking out of the church or of not opening the door ever crossed his mind.

He had no idea why he was here, but the thought reverberated in his mind. *Open the door.*

He pulled the door open slowly. The hinges creaked, growing in amplitude as the door opened. Kirk looked inside trying to adjust his eyes to the darkness inside the small room.

A noise like the low growl of a lion pierced the quiet of the church as two large glowing eyes opened before him. He screamed as he stumbled backwards, attempting to gain any distance between him and the door before falling to the floor.

Debris filled the air as the small room exploded around him. Kirk looked up from the dust to see a dragon standing over him. The dragon was just as he had seen in many of the books he had read. The arms were scaly up to where his pointy, ivory-like claws protruded, gleaming.

The dragon's height was enormous. Its head was larger than the size of Kirk's entire body, reaching almost all the way to the church ceiling twenty feet above them. His wings remained tucked against his body as the space in the church would not allow him to stretch them to their full mass. The dragon's tail snaked back into what was left of the tiny room. He lowered his head until Kirk could feel his hot breath on his cheeks. The dragon opened his mouth to reveal large, sharp teeth.

He's so big. It was the only thought Kirk's mind could ponder, as he stood dwarfed by the monster.

The dragon took a deep breath in through two large nostrils and paused for what seemed like an eternity, and then he exhaled. The wind blew through Kirk's hair, strong enough to make him take a step backward to maintain his balance.

"Fear...I can smell it on you." The dragon's eyes glowed more intensely.

"Wh-what do you want?" Kirk's voice trembled.

"To defeat you and take your soul, or should I say cause you to defeat yourself. As you grow older, you will find it harder to stay on the path of the righteous." The dragon's tone became sarcastic. "Clean your room, don't fight with your sister, don't cheat at school."

The dragon lowered his head to let Kirk look him in the eye and fear him. "DO YOU THINK IT'S ALWAYS GOING TO BE THAT EASY, THAT BLACK AND WHITE?" Kirk's hair blew in the warm breeze of the dragon's breath. "Ha! You may be able to fight temptation now, but as you grow older, I grow stronger and harder to defeat."

The dragon stood straight up, readying himself to strike, exposing his underside to Kirk.

Kirk remembered a book he had read about an older knight teaching a squire to defeat a dragon.

"Look for the weak spot underneath the dragon and strike it with your sword," explained the brave knight who had fought many dragons in his time. "That is where the dragon's weakness is."

A quick glance and Kirk spotted it, nearly seven feet from the ground.

"Harder, but not impossible," replied Kirk as he ran toward the dragon, jumping off a pew to gain the height and momentum he needed to bury his sword into the dragon's soft underbelly. The dragon screamed as he fell back into the room, tearing the remaining portion of the wall to the ground.

Kirk amazed himself. He was terrified and yet he stood his ground in the face of the beast.

As brave as the knight in my book, he thought to himself.

"I'll see you again, Kirk," moaned the dragon as he slumped to the ground.

"Kirk! Wake up, Kirk. You're going to be late."

Kirk raised his head from the pillow and looked at the clock.

7:15. Wow. I was sleeping good. Mom usually turns the light on at 6:45.

John, his brother, who had given him the wake-up call, was dressed and heading out of their bedroom for breakfast. Kirk immediately jumped from bed, feeling a rush from the courage he had shown in his dream. As he ran down the stairs, he was able to discern by the pleasant aroma that filled the house that they were having sausage and pancakes for breakfast.

"Good morning, Kirk," said his mom, smiling as she crossed from the table to the sink to begin the task of washing up after cooking the large breakfast.

"Pass me the syrup."

"You need to say please," sneered his sister Madeline as she stuck her tongue out at him.

"Just pass me the syrup, or I'm going to pass you my whole plate in your lap—food and all."

"Kirk, just say please," his mother asserted, shaking her head.

"Please," he grumbled.

"Now say thank you," stated Madeline with a hint of sarcasm in her voice.

"Madeline, that's enough." Her mom's smile never faded.

"John, can you take care of my chores today?" asked the oldest brother Jim as he picked up two pieces of sausage and headed out the door.

"That's the third time this week," complained John.

"I'm busy with extra morning practices for basketball. Gotta be ready for state this year, little bro. I apologize for those of you in the family who were not gifted with as much athletic ability as I, but we all need to make sacrifices so I can lead the team to state." Jim smiled as he headed out the door.

He does seem to be more athletic than the rest of the family, thought Kirk, who looked up to Jim despite his arrogance.

A loud roaring motor could be heard coming into the drive.

"Uncle Robert's here!" shouted Kirk, able to tell it was his uncle Robert's truck by the distinguishable sound the engine made.

His mom looked up from the dishes through the window above the sink and shook her head disapprovingly as her younger brother threw an empty beer can in with many others that lined the bottom of his pickup's bed. She smiled as the usual chaos that came with a visit from Uncle Robert could already be felt in the room as the kids ran to the door, leaving their half-full plates at the table.

"Don't forget to finish your breakfast! You guys need to be ready for school in thirty minutes."

"Run, you little devils!" screamed Robert in a threatening voice as he opened the door. "Run!"

"Oh, Robert," Madeline pointed out with a disgusted tone. "You know we're all getting too old to run from you, except Kirk."

Kirk stopped halfway to the living room as he heard the comment. He slowly walked back to the group with his head down, hoping no one would say anything else about the matter.

"I guess you are getting big, Madeline. So big that you don't even call me uncle anymore, but not so big that I can't whip you."

Robert's brown eyes lit up as he grabbed Madeline and threw her over his shoulder. The house was now out of control with the kids screaming and Uncle Robert growling as he chased the children with Madeline hanging over his shoulder.

"Robert, have you been drinking already?" asked Kirk's mom after the excitement died down.

"It's not just for breakfast anymore, Sis."

"You need to slow down, or you'll end up an old drunk like Uncle Fred. Remember how bad it was for his kids?"

"I don't have kids."

"You're too hard to talk to," she said as she turned away.

"Kirk, you up for some fence fixing this weekend?"

"You bet," replied Kirk, excited at the thought of going to work on Uncle Robert's farm.

"You can come along too, John."

"I've got plenty to do around here, thanks."

"See you this weekend, Kirk. I'll come by to pick you up around 6:30."

Robert walked out the door, leaving his sister to try to get the excited kids to finish their food and leave for school on time.

CHAPTER 2

Sarah Horton opened the door of her home with a burst of energy. "I'm home!" she shouted.

Sarah was having her seventeenth birthday today, and her dad had promised to take her to a Melon Head concert in the nearby town of Break Ridge despite the fact it was a Thursday night. "A school night, young lady," she envisioned her father saying.

Sarah had lived in Lansing all of her life and could not wait until graduation to move out. Being the daughter of the man who employed almost everyone in town had a distinct disadvantage when it came to relationships at school.

The large room she entered remained quiet. She flipped a light switch to the side of the door that lit up an impressive-looking crystal chandelier that hung eighteen feet above the highly polished marble floor. A wooden staircase with decorative spindles gently curved upward toward a landing that was near eye level with the bottom of the chandelier. Her greeting was not returned. She knew her mother would be gone this evening.

She couldn't miss her Thursday night at the bridge club, thought Sarah to herself. *Gossiping old bats.*

Her mom was always too busy being socially active with the town's upper crust to spend time doing family things.

"Hello?"

A feeling of disappointment grew inside of her as she realized her dad had not made it home from work.

I should have known, she thought to herself. *I wish I was as important to him as that factory.*

Sarah looked at the answering machine. The light was blinking to indicate a message had been left.

"Wonder who that is?" remarked Sarah sarcastically.

"Hey, Sarah," said the voice on the machine, "I'll have to cancel our plans for the concert tonight. Something came up at work, and I can't get away. I'll make it up. Sorry."

"Damn it, Dad!" shouted Sarah. "I'm not even going to try anymore. You always break our plans."

All Sarah wanted was to spend some time with him, and he always managed to disappoint her. She felt herself wanting to cry.

"I'm not crying. You're not worth it!" she shouted at her father as though he were there.

I can't even tell you how big a disappointment you are because you're never here. The thought angered her even more. They had planned this night for over a month, yet he broke the plans for something last-minute that came up at work.

She understood her father owned the factory and most of the town, but he was so bent on the "empire he built" that he found no time for his daughter and her life had suffered for it. She put her jacket back on and headed out the door for a walk.

CHAPTER 3

Kirk stopped to admire the sunset as the warm May breeze blew gently against his skin. Several different species of birds were serenading their mates, creating what sounded like a well-orchestrated symphony. He stood near a large wooden barn that from its design looked to have been built close to a century before. Despite its fading paint, it held an appearance of sturdiness which stood as a monument to the quality of the workmanship.

From this vantage point, Kirk could see cattle grazing in the pasture. Beyond the pasture was a large oak timber located in the floodplain of the sinew creek. The sun was setting behind the trees. A cloud drifted above the sun, scattering the sun's rays across the sky and causing an orange glow behind the cloud. A mist began to rise to the top of the trees, adding an otherworldliness to the scene and creating a temporary portrait Kirk found himself unable to turn away from until the sun was gone.

He had suffered through the last day of school for the week with a hangover from the night before and was feeling better now that he was doing the chores and working off what little remained of it. He and John were almost finished with the chores, and he was anxious to clean up and go to town for his Friday night date with Sarah. Sarah had turned seventeen the day before, and Kirk was taking her out for a special birthday dinner.

In general, he considered his communication ability to be a short-coming, but Sarah was the exception. Letting her know how he felt was not only something he could do, it was easy. There was no apprehension.

He had big plans for them when graduation came.

"We'll move to a big city," he told her with a gleam in his eye. "I'll get a job, while you work on your degree."

He was uncertain what he wanted to do for a living. The only part of the plan missing was deciding which big city. Kirk was hoping for New York, while she was looking for somewhere a little warmer such as Miami. New York or Miami—that was the dream. Sarah had a medical degree to pursue, and he decided that when the time came, he would find something to do.

Sarah had expressed a little concern at which profession he wished to choose, but she always stood by him on his dreams. She loved the way he would describe their life in the city. It sounded perfect to her.

"Race you to the house," hollered John, who was already running towards home with a good twenty-foot head start.

They both stood five eleven, although each claimed to be taller than the other. They both had sandy blond hair and blue eyes as well, but despite their physical similarities, their personalities were much different.

John seemed content with life on the farm, almost as though there was never another choice in life but to become a farmer. It seemed to Kirk that John could not grasp the concept of leaving this place, as though there was no world worth knowing beyond the farm. Kirk, on the other hand, couldn't wait to get on to more exciting things.

"There's something over that hill besides the local feed store," he would tell John. "Something past that is where I belong."

"What did you do to your truck?" asked John, pointing to the rear fender that had been bent as though something came at it from straight underneath.

Kirk thought back to the night before but could not remember hitting anything quite that hard. He remembered going to the car wash to wash the mud off so his mom wouldn't see how much mud he had been in. *I don't even remember driving home.*

John could tell from the pause and the confused look that Kirk could not remember making the dent.

"Damn it, Kirk. You've got to stop getting so drunk all the time. You do it almost every night. You're turning out just like Uncle Robert. Do you even remember driving home?"

"Yeah, I remember driving home. I wasn't that drunk," lied Kirk.

"What time did you make it home?" countered John.

"Around 12:30," he responded in an uncertain tone.

"Try 2:00. Good guess, though."

"I don't drink that much," said Kirk walking away, hoping he would drop the conversation.

I do hate that dent in my truck, he thought with a sharp twinge of regret. *Probably was looking up to Uncle Robert that got me started drinking. He gave me my first drink when I was twelve and quite a few since then.*

Upon entering the house, they were greeted by the smell of supper on the stove. Their mom always had a meal prepared for them just like clockwork.

"Sit down, boys," said their mom. "Dinner's ready."

"Mom, you know I'm taking Sarah out for her birthday tonight," replied Kirk.

Taking her out on Friday night was nothing new. Him and Sarah had an ongoing agreement that Friday night would be their night together and Saturday would be open to hang out with friends should they so choose.

"I'm taking Sarah out to eat like I have for the past who knows how many Fridays," said Kirk.

"You should invite her over to eat some Friday. I always cook more than enough."

Kirk knew she liked to cook and clean house to keep her mind occupied. It had only been a year and a half since his father had passed away, and his mom was still adjusting to her new life without him.

"Sometime soon, Mom," replied Kirk as he headed for the shower. He was always a little apprehensive about taking Sarah out to the farm. He liked the time they shared alone and did not want to spend "their" Friday night with anyone but her.

*　*　*

"See ya, Mom!" hollered Kirk as he walked out the door. "You, too, butthead," he said laughingly to John.

Kirk jumped in the truck his mom bought for him only recently. *Nice dent,* he thought to himself.

His dad had been foresighted enough to leave the family with a little money in the event of his passing. Kirk told his mom she didn't have to buy the truck for him, but she insisted, saying, "It would make your father happy to see you in it."

It was a couple of years old but nicer than what most kids were driving in his school.

He drove up the winding asphalt driveway to Sarah's house. The driveway was lined with well-tended ornamental trees and shrubs. The Horton's home was a large white mansion with a porch fronted by four impressive-looking columns. The front door was large enough Kirk was almost certain he could drive a small car through it.

He always hated going into the house. Her father was all business and was always inquiring as to what Kirk was going to do with his life. He was an overbearing successful businessman in his late fifties.

"Be a leader, son," he would tell Kirk. "That's the only way you'll be successful. Don't be a follower. Let the followers work for you."

Kirk had always been afraid to mention his career uncertainty to Sarah's father.

"Good evening, Mr. Horton. Is Sarah ready?" asked Kirk.

"Not yet, son," replied Mr. Horton. "Sit down for a minute, Kirk."

A chill ran up Kirk's spine. He hated being alone with Mr. Horton. "Okay, sir," he said, forcing his voice not to crack.

"What are you going to do with your life, son?" inquired Mr. Horton, putting his hand on the back of Kirk's neck.

Two things about this offend me, thought Kirk. *One, he's touching me; and two, I'm not his son.*

Kirk tried to hold back any appearance of being offended for two reasons. One was Sarah, and the other was Mr. Horton's size. He was a big man with the ability to intimidate. Kirk always thought that was one of the key factors to Mr. Horton's success.

"Well, sir," stammered Kirk. "I'm planning on—"

"Are you ready to go?" interrupted Sarah.

Sarah looked at Kirk with a knowing smile. She was always saving him from these moments with her father but not until he was very uncomfortable. He always teased her that she waited until the last possible minute.

Sarah was an attractive girl with dark eyes and black hair that seemed to flow with her movements. *Being with her the rest of my life must be how John feels about the farm,* thought Kirk. *There just isn't anything else.*

"We'll continue this conversation later, son," insisted Mr. Horton.

OK, dad, thought Kirk.

"Yes, sir," he replied instead.

It always made him more at ease to crack a joke in his head when he was uncomfortable. *My only defense is my humor.*

Sometimes it was hard for him to say what he was thinking to others. He often felt as though he was missing out on a lot of things because he never defended himself. Parents who taught Christian values had raised him, and the "turn the other cheek" philosophy seemed to have stuck with him.

Always mild mannered, he thought.

One of his friends told him he was timid. Kirk thought at least that sounded better than some of the other names he had heard for it. Sarah, on the other hand, made him feel strong, like a man. She understood him and what he was feeling and knew just what to say to boost his ego.

"Did ya miss me?" asked Sarah as she scooted over to sit beside him. She always waited until they were out of the driveway before sitting by him.

"Let's put it this way," replied Kirk with a smile, "I'm glad I held out for the bench seats instead of the bucket seats."

Sarah smiled at the comment.

"Well, son, what are you going to do with your life?" joked Sarah in a voice meant to imitate her father's.

"Hey! You WERE waiting for the last minute to rescue me!"

"What do you mean?" asked Sarah, giving the best innocent look she could.

"Are you ready for a beer?" asked Kirk, reaching under the seat for the beer he left there earlier so he could start drinking as soon as they left the Horton house.

"No, thanks."

Kirk opened his beer and chugged nearly half of it before taking a breath.

"What would please my lady for her dining pleasure tonight?"

"The usual," answered Sarah with a gleam in her eye.

The usual consisted of a local fast food burger, fries, and beer taken to the top of Lookout Hill. Most travelers through the area thought it must have a good view to get that nickname, but the hill received its moniker from the flocks of bird that nested there and were famous for "bomb droppings." The view of the landscape was poor, but the locals liked to send travelers up there as a joke. Kirk and Sarah enjoyed the area at night because the birds were in their nests and visitors to the site was rare.

Kirk laid a blanket on the ground past the edge of the area the birds flew over and sat down to enjoy their meal.

"Would you like a beer?"

"No, thanks," replied Sarah.

Kirk grabbed himself a beer.

"The stars are beautiful tonight."

"Do you think we're alone out here?" Sarah asked.

"I think so," answered Kirk. "Except for the birds."

"I mean life on other planets."

"I know what you meant, I was joking. I would have to say the odds are good for it. We've only been on one planet and it has life on it. So, I would say out of the other trillion or so planets we haven't been on, one of them is bound to have life. I love being here with you just talking and holding you."

"Me, too," replied Sarah warmly.

Kirk pushed her forward to allow himself to stand up.

"Ready for one yet?"

"No, thanks. Are you sure you need one?"

Kirk felt a little lightheaded from the beer he had consumed, but he wasn't ready to quit.

"I'm fine," replied Kirk trying not to slur his words. "Besides we still have an hour and a half until we have to leave. I only wish it was four hours," said Kirk, leaning over to kiss her. The look of concern left her as she surrendered to his warm kiss.

CHAPTER 4

Kirk drove down the winding trail back to town. It was 9:45 when he and Sarah had left Lookout Hill. Kirk had heard mention of a party on old Menlow Bridge, which had been abandoned by the county and was a popular party spot for the local teens.

"We have time to stop and have one beer at the party, then we'll head home," insisted Kirk.

"Let's head home now. We're going to be pushing it if we drive to the other side of town and have to head back after we stop for a while," Sarah pleaded.

"Come on. We're only young once. Let's enjoy it."

*   *   *

"Hey, Leo!" Kirk yelled as he walked towards the group of twenty or so kids.

Leo and Kirk had been friends since Kirk had enrolled in the local public high school after his "tour of duty" as Leo jokingly called it at the Catholic grade school. Kirk always teased back that some were meant to be tougher than others.

"How ya doing?" replied Leo as they exchanged a sort of secret series of combination handshakes and high fives. "Need another one?" asked Leo, pulling a cold beer out of his pocket.

"That's my brand!" exclaimed Kirk, sounding surprised. "Where did ya get that from?"

"Found it in the ditch," answered Leo with a wink.

It was considered to be dishonorable to reveal one's buyer amongst the students at Lansing High School.

"Hey, Leo. Do you want to go have some fun with me?"

"Kirk, this is Tiffany Johnson. Tiffany, this is Kirk."

"Nice to meet you." Kirk extended his hand to the petite blonde.

One of the cutest smiles Kirk had been fortunate to witness crossed her face. Her blue eyes glowed as though she had never been more excited to meet someone.

"Nice to meet you, Kirk."

Leo always was more tempting to the gorgeous ones. Should have found myself an uglier friend so I would be the best looking one. Sarah sees it differently though, Kirk thought to himself as he turned to see Sarah talking to one of her friends. A smile crossed his face as she turned and winked at him.

"It's time to go. I'm going to be late," emphasized Sarah as soon as he finished his third beer since arriving at the party.

Kirk looked at his watch.

"10:35. I better go, Leo. Looks like I could be late getting Sarah home."

Don't want my buddies to think I'm worried about getting her home late, but I really don't want to cross Mr. Horton.

"Are you okay to drive?" quizzed Sarah in a concerned voice.

"I'm fine," Kirk insisted, trying not to slur his words.

Kirk shifted the truck into reverse. His foot pushed into the gas pedal, increasing their speed.

"Slow down."

"I'm alright. Don't wor—"

"OHHH!"

The truck stopped instantly, bouncing the back end of the truck off the ground. Kirk looked at Sarah with a broad grin.

"OOPS."

"Let me drive, Kirk."

"I'm fine. I just didn't see the tree."

"Please, let me drive."

He started down the gravel road and turned on the highway. Kirk fought back the feeling of sleepiness, his mind focused on staying awake and getting Sarah home by 11:00.

Man, I did have quite a bit to drink, he thought to himself as he became aware of the magnitude of his intoxication. *I've got to get her home fast.*

He forced his head to stay up and fought to keep his eyes open as he drove down the road.

"Kirk, you're swerving. Pull over and let me drive," expressed Sarah with a note of fear in her voice.

"I'm okay. See, I'm doing fine," said Kirk as he leaned over to playfully kiss her, trying to lighten the mood.

"KIRK!" Sarah screamed as the truck left the road. The cool night air was filled with the sound of shattering glass and bending metal as the truck rolled down an embankment coming to rest on its top.

CHAPTER 5

Ron Truitt walked down Sanford Street in Binesford, Idaho, toward a small run-down trailer house he had started renting a month and a half ago. The old house was one of ten situated in the small trailer court. Many old items that should have been sent to the landfill months ago lay discarded around the small lot the trailer sat on. A blue Monte Carlo, sitting on blocks with license plates that had expired nearly a year and a half before, was parked in the driveway. From the junk that was stacked around the car, it was apparent no one had been in it for some time. The trailer itself showed many signs of neglect. The electricity had been shut off for two months, giving a passerby the appearance that this place was most likely abandoned.

Rotten place to live, thought Ron to himself. *Can't beat the fifty bucks a month though.*

His appearance closely reflected the neglected look of his mobile home. His face had not been shaved for a couple of weeks and may not have been washed in half that amount of time. His clothes had not been washed in two weeks and most likely had been slept in several times.

I hope I can pay the rent this month. Unemployment just doesn't pay good enough.

It was two months since being fired for testing positive on a drug test. Half of his unemployment check had been spent in the last week on drugs.

Ron opened the door to a place resembling the yard with items of no value cluttering the floor. The kitchen table was filled with empty boxes and old cans that remained half full. A thick, red-colored liquid was slowly dripping from the table.

The kitchen sink was full of dishes that would only be washed if someone had a need to use something.

Ron looked at his wife sitting in a rocking chair surrounded by various items that had been recklessly discarded. Her appearance indicated she had not slept for a long time; tired brown eyes seemed to beg for a single moment of rest, just a short rest from her life. Once a vibrant woman, she remembered walking down the bridal aisle full of hope for what was ahead of her. Now she sat in the middle of a pile of trash with two hungry children, her spirit broken, wondering how her life had come to this.

In her arms was a one-year-old baby, crying from lack of food. A second child who looked about two or three years old sat playing on the floor with a hairbrush. The child wore only a diaper that had not been changed for some time.

An involuntary sigh and slumping shoulders added to her broken appearance as she noticed his hands were empty.

"Ron, where are the diapers and milk?"

A look crossed his face that showed he had forgotten.

"Oh, Ron. Did you buy more drugs? How are we going to buy food and pay the rent? We have to stop living like this."

"Are you blaming ME for this? You could do something once in a while too. Why don't you get the damn milk?" he shouted, sounding angry, mostly caused by his mind wanting to get to the bedroom to take care of his addiction.

He was able to ignore her, but the screaming from his mind was impossible to block out. She stood in front of him, blocking his passage to the bedroom. "It has to stop, Ron. We can't live like this. The kids can't live like this."

Her plea failed to overcome the urging his mind was giving him to go back and snort the cocaine he had purchased with money that needed to be spent on food and diapers.

"GET OUT OF MY WAY!" he bellowed, pushing her.

She fell backward with a look of terror on her face. She tried to hang onto the baby but lost her grip as her head hit the chair. Ron looked as scared as Nancy as her eyes met his. He knew deep down he was not taking care of his family the way he should. He kept telling himself he would get off the drugs or that it wasn't really a problem. This was the first time it became physical. He had never laid a hand on Nancy or the kids before.

Nancy picked up the baby who was crying but seemed to be uninjured and held him to her shoulder.

"Go away. GET THE HELL AWAY FROM ME!" she shouted in a trembling voice as she glared at Ron with a look that gave no indication she was open to discussion.

Ron turned and walked out the door.

CHAPTER 6

Ron spent the night on the east side of Binesford in an abandoned ware-house commonly used by the homeless and drug users and dealers. The police occasionally raided the place—mostly to ask questions in a case they were working on. The police's mood seemed to be that if the activity was kept in the warehouse they were willing to look the other way.

Ron had snorted enough coke to forget about his wife and kids for the night, but with the morning came the memory of the night before. *Shouldn't have done that,* he thought with a twinge of guilt. *I can make it up to her later. Today will be my last day with the drugs, and then I'll make a new start tomorrow.*

Ron grabbed what was left of his cocaine and snorted another line. The twinge of guilt left him. "That's better. You always make me feel better," he said with a laugh, looking at what little cocaine was left in the bag.

"Get some milk and diapers," he mocked in a sarcastic tone. "I got what I need," he said, referring to the bag of coke.

I'm going to have a talk with her. She can't talk to me like that. It's not my fault I got fired. I'm doing everything I can. She acts like I don't try.

He made his way back to the trailer park determined to make Nancy understand how hard he tried and that it wasn't his fault. It was bad luck, and he would get them out of it.

"Nancy?" he declared loudly as he opened the door.

No answer.

"Nancy, I'm home."

The trailer remained quiet.

Ron searched the trailer only to find it abandoned.

I'll just fix me something to eat and wait, thought Ron, not realizing it had been almost sixteen hours since he had eaten.

He walked to the refrigerator. As he grabbed the handle he saw a note stuck to the front with a magnet.

Ron,

I've taken the kids and I am leaving you. Until tonight I held hope we could work through your drug problems. I realized tonight that both of us have to want it, not just me. I was scared tonight, scared for our children and myself. We can't live like this. I am taking the kids and you will never have a chance to see them again. I would let you know where we are if I wasn't so afraid of you. I don't know who you are. Five years of marriage and it occurred to me tonight that I don't know you.

Ron's feeling that he would convince his wife how hard he was trying to change things turned to the realization he had failed. Not only had he failed, but he failed to try. Failed to realize what he was putting her and the kids through. The letter seemed so strange to him. It was written to someone who considered him a stranger. He realized after reading the letter that the woman he knew so well five years ago was in fact a stranger to him. He couldn't comprehend how things had come to this point.

How did it get so bad so quickly?

Then the realization he may never see his children again hit him.

"No. NO!" he screamed as he kicked over the kitchen table, knocking old magazines and boxes off the table onto the already cluttered floor.

CHAPTER 7

The conference room on the upper floor of the J&R McCarry building gave clients the impression they were dealing with a class act company who wanted only the best. The large oak tabletop held the mirrored image of the room. The chairs surrounding the table matched the oak finish of the table with a fancy trim on the backs of the chairs and the highly polished look of all the furniture.

At the backside of the room away from the entrance sat two men at a moderate-sized bar meant for entertaining clients. Tonight, one of the two men at the bar was Jeff McCarry, CEO of J&R McCarry Inc.

Jeff was a tall man with a broad build and bright blue eyes full of energy. He had been with J&R since the beginning. He was J&R, since his brother Robert had died an untimely death of a heart attack a few years back. Now Jeff held controlling interest in the company.

J&R was the largest construction company on the East Coast. They worked on projects ranging from football stadiums to the twenty-one-story Labell Tower in Miami. J&R began as a moderate construction company working with residential housing and single-story buildings in rapidly developing areas of Virginia. Jeff remembered starting the company with his brother after the construction company they had worked for filed for bankruptcy.

"What are we going to do? That's what I asked Robert," Jeff told Sam Grishman, who was sitting across the bar from him.

The company had hired Sam for his vast experience with larger construction projects. He worked as a foreman for one of the largest construction companies at the time and was enticed by Jeff and Robert to come work for them. Sam was licensed as a structural engineer whose skill with design work was second only to his love of being on site coaching the men until they were a perfectly orchestrated team adept at nearly any task put before them.

Now Sam sat in front of Jeff . . . about to hear a story he had heard almost every time he and Jeff sat in this room alone. *He's not half the businessman his brother was,* he thought to himself, missing the days when Robert ran the company.

Jeff knew how Sam felt about him. That was one of his best qualities. He knew what people were thinking and what they wanted to hear.

"We wouldn't have made it without you onboard, Sam."

Sam was one of the few people who knew Jeff too well to fall for his lies and was growing tired of the dishonest lengths he would go to just to keep the company running.

"We need to start our own business. That's what he told me. I wouldn't have dreamt for a million years it would succeed. Fifteen years later and here I am CEO of my own company that's going to be declaring bankruptcy if we don't find a couple of high-profit jobs to pull us out of the frying pan."

"You don't think I feel the same way?" exclaimed Sam, sounding offended. "We both want this company to succeed. Me, so that my guys will have a place to work, and you because it fattens your wallet. You forget the company is more than this building. More than financial statements and quarterly records. It's men and women out there who take pride in what they build. All you care about building is your bank account. You used to be one of those guys, Jeff. What the hell happened to you?"

"I remember what it's like out there," Jeff debated, trying to defend himself even though most of what Sam said was true. Jeff was detached enough from the work outside the office that it was all about the money coming in.

Who can we bill? How much? When is the next stockholder meeting?

Jeff was faced with the sad truth that he didn't set foot on a job site these days unless the client requested it.

"If I didn't take care of the finances, there wouldn't be a company here for your guys to work at. You've even helped me come up with less than ethical ways to make payroll, and if the stockholders found out what our real situation was both of us would be in prison. Whether we like each other or not, we both have too much dirt on each other not to see it through."

"I KNOW," Sam replied as mad at himself as he was at Jeff for letting himself get involved in his half-baked schemes to convince the stockholders the company had more value than it did.

"You could at least show up on the job sites and let the guys know you think they're doing a good job. Robert used to. It builds up the morale."

"I don't need you to compare the way I run this company to the way Robert used to," Jeff said in a stern tone. "What are we gonna do about finding some projects?" he said, trying to get off a subject he didn't care to deal with.

"Word is there's a large hydroelectric dam project getting ready to bid in Tennessee on the Plymouth River. Mostly funded by the feds. Engineer estimated it to be somewhere around thirty billion. Has a four-year deadline on it. Sounds like just what we need to get back on our feet."

"Any other companies in the running for it?"

"I talked to the engineer on the project, had a couple classes with him in college. Hard to get much out of him about the other contractors looking at it, but it sounds like Wentworth construction out of Chicago might be interested in it."

Jeff looked at him with a raised eyebrow.

"They have a real shot at it. Young company trying to expand. They probably don't have the overhead we do."

"What are our options?" Jeff asked somberly.

Sam looked around the room to make certain they were alone.

"Blackmail or bribe. We don't stand a chance."

"Damn!"

Jeff remembered back when his company was bidding on some of the bigger projects and larger companies came in trying to bully them out of the running. Back then it seemed so easy not to give into the bullying or the bribing. There was nothing to lose. Now there were stockholders, board members, and employees with families he had to answer to. It felt good when the big dogs came in bullying and standing up to them to get the job.

"Sure is a lot easier to do what's right when it makes a profit. Do we have enough to bribe our way into this job?" Jeff inquired with an unsure tone.

"It would take ten million to bribe a dishonest contractor off the job, and I would still say they would want to be in on a fair amount of the subcontractor work. Wentworth is hungry to expand. They won't leave easy."

"Damn, we can't do that. I don't think we would finish this month's payroll out if we did unless we can shake some money loose out of our accounts receivable."

"I know," Sam mumbled in a flat tone. "That leaves us one option."

Jeff brushed his hand through his hair as though he were trying to think of some other way out, even though he had already decided blackmail would be his course of action. They had done this before, and each time it became easier. The first time they blackmailed a contractor out of bidding a job, Jeff spent what seemed like weeks without sleep. He had compromised his integrity. Now, he would lay awake maybe fifteen minutes thinking about it before he fell asleep and never looked back.

Find the man who turned the bids in for the company. Hire a private investigator to do a background check on him. It was simple. Was he embezzling company money? Was he cheating on his wife? Find out his secret. He could still turn in the bid, but he would fill out the bid form with a price that was given to him, leaving the job to the only other company capable of a project this size. Jeff smiled at the thought.

"Now we need to find out who at Wentworth is putting together the bid and what his background is," Jeff stated with a knowing nod to Sam.

"I've got our man on it."

Jeff watched him walk out of the room. *Don't get caught,* thought Jeff with a gleam in his eyes.

CHAPTER 8

Mike Hollister sat at his desk in his small office infested with rolled-up plans in boxes bound only by rubber bands. A three-foot-wide path from his door was the only means of accessing his desk.

Mike enjoyed his work. Thirty-three years old and single, it was all he had. He often brought his work home to give himself something to keep him from going nuts from the emptiness of his sparsely furnished, lifeless house.

"I got some more plans for you to add to your pile," said a well-dressed attractive woman who appeared to be in her early forties.

Mike glanced up from his computer.

"Good morning, Gloria. I hope that's the Plymouth Dam plans we ordered."

"It sure is. Make sure you take a good look at 'em. A project like that would be good for Wentworth and probably wouldn't hurt your resume or paycheck either. If you get the project, I might treat you to lunch sometime," she said with a smile as she left the room.

Mike disregarded comments such as those because they did not contribute to the process of completing any work task he had on his mind and therefore he viewed them as a waste of time.

He cleared his desk to allow room to roll the plans out for better viewing.

Can't believe I'm this excited about bidding a job. Feels almost like the first one I ever bid. Darn sure is the biggest, he thought, barely able to contain his excitement enough to focus on any single part of the plans.

Mike had been hired by Wentworth construction two years before and until now had only been allowed to manage smaller construction projects, even though at his previous company he had been on larger jobs. Now, Tim Wentworth took the company over from his father and was looking to expand. Tim, who did not have the construction sense of his father, was a keen enough businessman to know he needed to hire someone who understood the construction business and could bid the bigger projects they would need if the company was to expand.

After about ten minutes of wildly looking through the plans and not retaining any of the information he viewed, Mike sat down with a notebook and began the tedious task of converting what he read on the plans into man-hours, equipment, and materials plus profit.

Don't blow this one, Mike ol' boy. This is what you've been waiting for. If you can pull this off, you're going to be in a very good position with one of the fastest growing construction companies in the country.

Focus on the plans, he thought to himself, trying to pull his dreams back into reality.

CHAPTER 9

Jeff sat at the bar in the conference room at J&R. It was 10:30 in the evening. *Wonder what Sam wants now. Must be important to have a meeting this late.*

Jeff knew a late meeting meant something was happening that as few people as possible at the company needed to know about. He poured himself a scotch and water, and out of habit poured a rum and Coke for Sam.

It's funny. We both hate each other, but if he got here before I did, he would have a drink ready for me, Jeff laughed as he thought about his relationship with Sam. No matter how much things had changed, they were both men of habits they had started a long time ago when they used to respect each other. Some old gestures still continued.

Robert, how come people liked you so much better than me? This company would still be stable if you were here. You got the employees to do what we needed them to do, while I was better at dealing with the people outside the company.

"He's clean," announced Sam, bursting into the room.

Jeff jerked, startled by the sudden interruption.

"What are you talking about?"

"Mike Hollister with Wentworth. He's our bid man." Sam threw a manila folder down on the bar.

"This is all our P.I. could come up with?"

"He could only come up with dirt on one employee in the whole company. Hollister's squeaky clean. Minus the missions to third-world countries, this guy's a saint. Goes home after work. Eats out of the microwave, watches old re-runs, then goes to bed. He seems to want to get in on the ground floor of Wentworth and float to the top as they grow."

"No chance of bribing him into messing up his bid?"

"The guy would be stupid to mess up his perfect bid record. He's yet to mess one up. Pays attention to the small details and understands the contract documents. The guy worked ten years as a laborer, three as a foreman, has taken every class there is that has anything to do with construction from legal aspects to construction management, and has been involved with numerous bids. I'm really not sure why the guy never started his own company," Sam stated almost as though he admired him.

"Mike Hollister," Jeff read from the file.

"He's got a history of good bids. Gets the project, makes a profit."

"What would it take to get him to work for us?"

"The P.I. indicated that was unlikely. He talked to some people who know Mike. He's motivated by his worth to a company. Wentworth is small. They need him if they're going to expand. He wants to see them grow. He feels like he would be lost in our corporate world. We just need to turn in our bid and hope for the best," said Sam, finishing his drink. "That's all we can do. I'm heading home. It's been a long day."

Jeff watched Sam as he walked out the door.

"I think we can do more," he whispered as he opened the detailed file from the private investigator. "You give up too easy."

CHAPTER 10

Sam walked toward the ten-story federal building in Nashville with his bid packet in hand. The sun was shining on the south side of the glass front of the building. The windows appeared to be free of any dirt as though they had been cleaned that morning.

Must have known I was coming, thought Sam. *Guess I know better than to think they cleaned the place up for me, but I can't help but feel good about this bid. I hope $35.1 billion will work. Wentworth might be able to beat that.*

Sam walked through a metal detector manned by a security guard he would have guessed was old enough to retire but probably didn't want to or couldn't afford to. The room beyond was large with marble floors, and a huge chandelier hung from the center of the dome-shaped ceiling he estimated must be twenty-five feet to the highest point. He always stopped to admire the construction when he walked into a building.

Marble was laid well, level corners come together nicely. The walls look like they might have been out of square by nearly three-quarters of an inch judging from the way the pattern of the marble did not run parallel to the trim at the wall. Happens sometimes, I guess. Good thing the inspector didn't know what he was looking at.

"Third floor," Sam read from the advertisement he'd been sent. "Tuesday January 15 at 1:00."

Sam looked at his watch. *Right place. Thirty minutes to spare . . . on time. Might as well head upstairs and see if anyone else decided to show up. Might want to raise my bid if I'm the only one here,* he thought to himself amusingly.

Sam walked into the large conference room. *They did it again. They build these new buildings and they furnish them with the oldest, ugliest furniture they can find,* he thought, looking at the old table in need of refinishing surrounded by chairs that would have looked more fitting in a building that was closer to fifty years old.

"Guess they're saving me tax money," he said to himself, giving his brain permission to stop critiquing the construction and the furnishings of the building and to introduce himself to the two people sitting at the table.

"Sam Grisham," he said, holding his hand out to the man across the table.

"Mike Hollister, Wentworth Construction."

Sam had intentionally left out the fact that he worked for J&R McCarry. *I remember when my name was Sam Grisham, J&R McCarry, but I'm not so proud of that fact any more. I'm just so tied up in bad dealings with Jeff I feel trapped.*

"Sam Grisham!" declared the middle-aged man sitting across the table. "Pleasure to finally meet you. I'm Jim Levell with Concord."

"Nice to meet you," responded Sam who was modestly accustomed to being recognized by his peers.

The room began to fill up with people ranging from officials with the governor's office to an elderly looking woman Sam was sure didn't have anything better to do than nose into the bid opening.

"I believe the official time is 1:00," announced Jim, looking for an approving nod from the governor's aide.

"For those of you who don't know me, I'm Jim Levell with Concord Engineering. I would like to thank all of you for showing up. We have two bids at this time and can no longer accept more. If there are no objections, I will open the bids."

He handles himself pretty well, thought Sam.

"The first bid is from J&R McCarry. Sam Grisham is here today to represent the company. Sam, good to have you with us."

"Good to be here, Jim."

Jim began to open the tightly sealed package from J&R. The opening was sealed with several layers of shipping tape.

"A sealed bid doesn't mean you need the keys to Fort Knox to get into it. It just means they have to be closed, gentlemen. You know I can't get my pocket knife through the metal detector downstairs."

The comment initiated a small wave of laughter.

"Thirty-five billion, one million, one hundred thousand dollars and zero cents. From J&R McCarry INC."

"Thirty-five billion, one million, one hundred thousand dollars and zero cents," repeated the woman in her late twenties from the governor's office after she wrote the figure down in her notes.

We lost it, thought Sam, noticing the subtle change in Mike's expression that indicated he was pleased.

Jim laid the packet down and grabbed the sealed envelope from Wentworth Construction.

"I'm glad to see you didn't wrap yours up so tight."

Mike's expression showed his true feelings as he seemed to enjoy the comment that allowed him to visually express the excitement he was feeling. Jim pinched the metal clips together and opened the folder.

"Thirty-six billion, five million, five hundred thousand dollars and zero cents. From Wentworth Construction Incorporated."

Sam watched Mike's expression change as though this was the first time he had heard the bid from his own company.

"Thirty-six billion, five million, five hundred thousand dollars and zero cents" was repeated.

"That's correct."

Mike looked like he was about to jump out of his seat and protest but thought better of it.

"Jim, can I take a look at that?" asked Mike.

"Is there a problem?"

"Just want to see it."

"Is that okay?" Jim said, looking at the governor's representative.

A slight nod from a well-dressed, arrogant-looking man gave the approval. Mike took the bid.

He's going to have a stroke. He's never even seen the bottom line of that bid, thought Sam, noticing the change in Mike's expression.

"Is there a problem?" asked Jim after several uncertain seconds.

Mike looked around the room. He had been so wrapped up in looking over the bid form he had forgotten he was sitting in this room with people waiting on him.

"No. It's all in order."

He knows if he says something's wrong he'll never be able to find a job in this line of work. Hope he doesn't say anything. Looks like he might pass out. Gotta be Jeff behind this.

CHAPTER 11

Jeff's office was quiet. He had not heard anything from Sam yet but felt reasonably certain J&R was the low bidder on the Plymouth River dam project.

"Mr. Levell on line two."

Jeff picked up the phone.

"This is Jeff."

"Mr. McCarry, I would like to congratulate you on your low bid for the Plymouth River dam project. Pending the funding agencies' and attorney approval, I look forward to working with you."

"Well, this is the first I heard we were the low bidder. Sam hasn't made it in yet, but I do appreciate the news."

"I've heard a lot of good things about your company, Mr. McCarry."

The door to the office opened quickly. Jeff could tell from past experience that Sam was in a bad mood and was about to tell him why. Jeff raised his hand and pointed to the phone to let Sam know he should wait until the call was done.

"Call me Jeff, and the same goes for Concord. I've heard a lot of good things," Jeff remarked, growing tired of these formalities that preceded every construction job he could remember.

"I just wanted to touch base with you and let you know the attorneys are reviewing the contract documents and we will be in touch with any comments or concerns they have."

"I appreciate that."

"We'll be in touch. Take care."

"See ya."

"You son-of-a-bitch. How the hell did you change his bid?"

Jeff took a breath to shift gears from the pleasant formalities he had exchanged with Jim to the anger he was hearing in Sam's voice.

"What the hell are you talking about? We got the bid square."

"You don't have to lie to me, Jeff. I know you got to him." Sam poked his finger hard into Jeff's chest.

"If I did get to him, why would that make you so mad? It wouldn't be the first person we got to."

"It would be the first clean one we got to. We didn't have jack on him."

The realization that he was so mad about getting to Mike because he was clean sunk in.

"Well, I'll keep our P.I. on him until he does something wrong if it'll make you feel better."

"He had us, Jeff. He had us fair and square. I don't know how you did it, but it was wrong. You crossed a line I can't make myself cross. He was clean. You can take your dam and build it yourself."

Sam grabbed Jeff's drink and threw it across the room, shattering it. A flash of anger crossed Jeff's face, turning his normally pale cheeks, bright red.

"You son-of-a—" Jeff quickly decided to hold his words as he could tell from Sam's steely glare and slight tremble in his hands that he wasn't going to back down on this one.

"He was clean. Like I used to be before you got to me. You're a virus, Jeff. You infect everyone you come into contact with."

"Think about your workers, Sam. They need you to pull them through this."

"You can find some other foreman to handle the job."

"I don't think you'll find another job with the information I have on you."

Sam walked out the door. Jeff was certain he would be back in the morning.

CHAPTER 12

Mike Hollister walked into his office and turned on the light. It was ten o'clock in the evening.

The office seems haunted this time of night.

A glazed look came to his eyes as he played back the events of the past twenty-four hours in his mind, trying to figure out who switched his bid form.

Had to be while I was out to lunch. I had the bid ready, came back, and it never left my side after that. Someone in the company. Has to be.

The thought had been in his mind that it was an inside job, but he wanted to make certain there wasn't another possible scenario before pointing fingers in the direction of his co-workers.

I need to check the computer, see if the electronic version is the old one. Don't know why I didn't think of that before. He logged on to his computer. *Start menu. Recent documents . . . Bid info.* He clicked the document open.

They changed it. They changed it on the computer and erased the old one. Wanted it to look like it was my mistake. Damn it. Why the hell did they do this? Who did it?

The backup on the server. Why didn't I think of that before?

The company used to have each computer set up individually but had decided that having a mainframe everyone was hooked into would pay for itself in time spent sharing folders. The automatic backup every night was icing on the cake after the loss of a couple of bid forms that had to be filled out by hand at the last minute on the way to the bid opening.

Mike went to a small room towards the rear of the office to a computer sitting on a small table, which made it impossible to use the computer comfortably.

Let's see now, I've seen our computer man, Jim, log on and look at the backup files a dozen times.

Mike viewed the folders that had been backed up from the day before. He surfed around the files until he came to the Plymouth dam folder at the same location he had found it on his computer, only here it was under a folder named "Backup."

"Bid info. Come on, be the right one," he said as he clicked to open the document.

Bingo.

It was the original document.

Now what am I gonna do with this information? I can save it to a disk, print it off, or maybe leave it here and show Tim, but what's that gonna prove? I could have changed my mind about the amount at the last minute. It would look better if I just said I bid too high than to try and blame someone else for this.

Mike walked back to his office and sat at his desk. He had been up for nearly twenty hours, and he was feeling overwhelmingly alone and frustrated.

Better think your way out of this. They were depending on this job. You told them you would get it. They can't afford to pay what they're paying you if you can't prove that you're not worth it.

Okay, forget about losing your job. Let's think about this with a more structured approach. I have the copy on the backup that I did; I have the copy in the current folder. I know someone else in the company did the revising. Now how am I going to find out who it was and prove it? There's only three other people in this office that could access those files. Now which one would be the main suspect?

A sick feeling grew in his stomach as he tried to picture which person he worked with every day who could do something to him that would, he was sure, cost him his job and possibly finish his chance at another job in this line of work.

Can't accuse anyone without proof, Mike. Let's have a look at that again. I think there's something I'm missing. Start menu. Recent documents. Bid info.

The document started to open.

Holy cow. Why didn't I think of that? They wouldn't have had to come into my office and change it on my computer; they would have changed it on theirs, printed it off, and would only have been in my office long enough to pull the old bid out and slip the new one in. If they didn't empty the recent documents, it will show up at their computer.

Excitement at the possibility of finding out who had done this filled him with a new energy.

Got to get the passwords, he thought to himself heading back to the room with the main frame.

The company had them put passwords on each computer, but given the fact Steve would often out of habit save folders to his hard drive, they decided to leave the passwords where the employees could find them if they needed to access one of the other computers.

Mike sat at Steve's computer first. He hated to think Steve, who seemed like a good dad to his three kids and a good husband to his wife, would be capable of something like this.

He would probably need the money the most if it was a bribe.

"Fatherofthree."

Clever password, Steve.

The computer opened to a background of a family photo with an attractive woman with brown eyes and black hair. The boy and one of the two girls in the picture shared the mother's black hair while the second girl had her father's blond hair.

Please don't let it be you, Steve. I'm sure I can't turn you in, he thought, looking at the little kids. *I've never had kids, but I'm sure I would do anything I could for them.*

Mike moved the cursor over to the start menu, recent documents.

Thank God, Mike thought to himself, relieved it did not show up on Steve's computer.

Mike logged off the computer and went to Roger's desk.

I know if you did it, Roger, it was just greed. Between you and your wife you probably take in over $200,000 a year. Should be more than enough to get by.

A feeling that Roger was the one who had done it suddenly came over him.

He does have a lot of monthly payments. The big house, two nice cars, a boat. Did you overextend yourself on payments? What did they offer you to screw up my life? Half a million or was it less?

The thought hadn't yet occurred to Mike about how much of a bribe would be offered to throw the bid on a project like this.

If I was dishonest and didn't enjoy this line of work, I could have made a one-time deal and been set up for a good while. Got to stop thinking like that. I'm not gonna do it so there's no reason to think about it. At least it got me off Roger's case for a little bit.

The computer opened up to a background that showed Roger's boat at the lake as he was pulling away from the dock.

Fitting. It is a nice boat, though.

Start, recent documents . . .

It's not there. Someone was smart enough to clear it out after they were done. Damn. Guess I should check Gloria's computer.

Mike tried to put the thought out of his mind, but he felt certain Roger was the one who did it.

He could be bought. Especially for the kind of money that would have been offered.

Mike walked to the front of the office near the entrance to Gloria's desk. Sorry, Gloria, but I have to check.

Mike opened the computer to the standard background that was probably the same one that came with the computer. Start, recent documents . . .

Gloria . . . why?

A sick feeling crept into his stomach.

I thought I would be glad to find out who did it. I think I'm going to throw up. Now what am I going to do?

CHAPTER 13

Gloria sat her two loaves of bread and carton of milk on the conveyor belt of the checkout line. The three open aisles were backed up with people who all were in a hurry and seemed irritated at the fifteen checkout lines that remained closed.

"Eighteen checkout lanes they advertised," commented the elderly gentleman in line behind her.

A smile was the only acknowledgment she gave him.

The young lady behind the register shot a glance to Gloria that seemed to convey something to the effect of "don't look at me, I just work here."

"Paper or plastic?"

After making the decision to go with plastic and paying her $5.52, Gloria made her way to her midsized red SUV. The vehicle's lights flashed and a quick beep of the horn gave her the indication she had successfully unlocked it. She reached for the rear door to put the groceries in.

"You're coming with me, Gloria. Don't do anything stupid."

The sharp jab in her back was enough to convince her the perpetrator meant business.

"The money's in my purse . . . take it."

"I don't want your damn money. I want answers."

She was spun around to see a face she had been afraid of seeing for the last two months. His hair, which now had a greasy unwashed look, was nearly two inches longer than the last time she saw him. The hair on his face indicated that might have been the last time he shaved. It took her an instant to even realize it was him. He had changed.

A chill ran down her spine as she realized this ungroomed man with a disturbing look in his eyes had a score to settle with her.

"I can tell by the look on your face you're happy to see me too."

"What do you want, Mike?"

"I want you to get in my vehicle now before I have to shoot you."

He rammed what Gloria was sure was a gun harder into her side.

"ALL RIGHT. All right. I'll get in."

Fear and uncertainty gripped her at the helplessness of the situation. She knew he would be mad at her and doubted she could talk her way out of making him believe she wasn't the one who changed the bid.

Gloria jumped in the passenger side of the vehicle. As Mike went to the driver's side, a voice in her head told her to jump out and run screaming for help. The panic and shortness of breath she felt gave her strong doubts it was a good idea.

"Who was it, Gloria? Who got to you?"

He's not even asking if I did it. He must know it's me.

"What are you talking about, Mike?"

"Don't play games with me. I spent the past two months trying to figure out where I was going to work and you know what?"

She sat and stared at Mike as his increasingly louder tone gave her the indication his temper was rising with it.

"DO YOU KNOW WHAT? ANSWER THE DAMN QUESTION! I'M TALKING TO YOU!" he said in an enraged voice, putting the gun to her temple.

"No. I don't know, I don't know!" she replied, nearly hysterical.

"I can't get a damn job anywhere. You set me up. You got paid big money, and you changed my bid."

Mike glanced out of the window to see someone coming out of the store toward him with a shopping cart. In the rage of the moment he had forgotten they were still at the store parking lot.

"We're gonna go somewhere a little more private and finish this. Don't do anything stupid," he said, holding the gun up off the seat for her to see.

"Who was it, Gloria? Who got you to turn on me?"

"I don't know, Mike. He never said his name."

"I thought you might say that. Look at this."

Mike handed her the current issue of *Engineering Monthly*.

"Check out page forty-three and see if anyone looks familiar."

She turned to the page and saw an article titled, "Plymouth Dam Project Awarded." Beneath was a picture of several people from McCarry Construction along with the engineer and a couple of government officials.

Gloria flinched. *It's him,* she thought as her eyes picked out Jeff McCarry.

"I've never seen any of these people."

It was too late. Mike caught her reaction. He pulled over into a quiet alley.

"Get the hell out of the truck."

Oh, my God. He's gonna kill me. Gloria almost stood up in the seat looking for a way to get out of the truck and run.

The door opened, and he abruptly pulled her out of the truck and let her fall hard onto the sparsely graveled alley. He put his knee onto her neck holding her down and forcing her to fight for each breath.

"Please, Mike," she choked.

She felt the end of the gun pressing against the side of her head. Mike shoved the magazine into her face.

"Which one is it? Point at him."

From the position she was in, she had to force her eyes sideways until they almost hurt to see the picture. She pointed at Jeff. The pressure let up immediately from her neck.

"Uhhhhhhh," she took a deep breath while grabbing her neck.

"This one?" he asked, pointing at Jeff.

A nod of her head answered the question.

"Jeff McCarry. You're gonna pay for ruining my life."

A sick feeling ran through Gloria as the realization sunk in that this man who was so obsessed with his work had no other outlet in his life and had turned his obsession towards vengeance. If he was as passionate about the vengeance as he was about the work, she was certain he would see this through.

CHAPTER 14

Jeff McCarry sat in his lavish home just outside the town of Rollings, Virginia. The one-story brick home nestled into the steep forest-covered hills overlooked the large Malkin River Valley. He sat in his recliner, surrounded overhead by many different mounts from the yearly hunting trips he enjoyed.

Jeff, you've pulled the company out of the fire again, he thought as he rattled the ice left in his shot glass. *Too bad you can't hold your relationships together as well as you can the company. Maybe if you weren't so obsessed with your work, you could.*

He finished his drink and walked over to the bar in the corner and filled his glass. A scratching sound from the back door told Jeff his dog was ready to come in.

"Hold on, Jim ol' boy. I'll open the door for you in a minute. Hmm, old rascal."

He finished pouring his drink and walked over to the back door. He reached for the door handle and paused.

"You should lock your doors, Jeff."

Jeff felt hard metal on the back of his neck. A chill ran down his spine at the thought of a loaded gun being pointed at him. He started to turn.

"Don't even think about it. Just walk outside and don't turn around."

Jeff and his assailant walked outside, across the driveway, and down the dusty road to where his van was parked.

"Who the hell are you?"

"Why don't you turn around and see if you recognize me?"

Jeff turned.

"I don't know you."

"You know me, you arrogant piece of crap. You at least know me from some file you read on me. I'm Mike Hollister."

Jeff looked hard. He had seen Mike's picture, but this man standing in front of him didn't fit the picture he had seen.

"What do you want from me?"

"You ruined my life. You took everything I worked for and threw it away. I had the bid. I had you, Jeff, and you took it away."

"I don't know what you're talking about," he said, trying to sound as innocent as the fear of the situation would allow.

"Does this refresh your memory?" Mike said, opening the side door of the van, revealing Gloria with her arms and legs bound in duct tape. Her eyes revealed a desire to scream in terror that the duct tape across her mouth would not allow.

"What have you do—"

A quick blow with the butt of the gun to the back of his neck cut off Jeff's words. Jeff dropped to the ground instantly.

"YES. THAT FELT GOOD. Did that feel good for YOU, Jeff?" he said, spitting uncontrollably into Jeff's unconscious face.

The fanatical look in his eyes was fueled by two months of obsession, contemplating what he would do to the person who was responsible. He felt alive, like this was the most right thing he ever did. Most of all, he felt vindicated.

CHAPTER 15

Jeff slowly opened his eyes. A sharp pain ran through his head. He tried to recall where he was or what had happened. His first thought was he went out and had partied too much. He looked around and saw trees.

I'm in a forest. Mike Hollister. The name brought back the memories of what had happened. He sat up and rubbed the back of his neck.

"Oh, wow."

He had never felt a pain that sharp before. He looked around to see the van from the night before about twenty feet away on a path he was surprised the van had been able to maneuver.

"MMmm . . . uhhhh."

Jeff turned to see Gloria still tied up only a few feet behind him. He made a quick survey of the area and decided no one else was around. He crawled on all fours over to Gloria and pulled the tape off her mouth.

"We've got to get out of here. He'll kill us."

Her words were no longer hysterical but came out matter-of-factly. She had been with Mike enough in the last twenty-four hours to have her emotions range from fear of dying, to certainty of dying, to survival at all costs.

Look for any opportunity to escape.

Despite the overwhelming odds, she felt a determination she never had before. Jeff heard the certainty in her words and quickly untied her.

"Let's go."

Jeff pulled her up, and they ran to the van. Gloria jumped in the passenger side, and Jeff hopped into the driver's seat.

"I can't believe he left the keys in it," he exclaimed, turning over the engine.

Jeff pulled the gearshift into drive and released the parking brake. The engine revved up as the vehicle rolled backwards.

"What the hell?" Jeff pushed on the accelerator only to have the engine rev louder as the vehicle gained momentum.

Jeff turned to Gloria who gave him an uncertain look at the predicament they had now found themselves in. The brakes didn't stop even though he had them pushed firmly against the floor.

"The brakes are out."

"The damn thing won't stop."

The thought of using the emergency brake entered his mind a split second too late as the van slammed into a large maple tree, stopping the van quicker than they would have liked. Gloria looked at Jeff as if to ask what else could go wrong.

"Doesn't work too good without this," said Mike suddenly appearing in Jeff's window.

In his left hand he held a drive shaft. In his right was the gun. A wave of despair ran through the captive pair as they realized their attempted escape had been a setup. Mike saw the look he had been waiting for.

"It doesn't feel good to have hope, only to have it taken away from you at the last minute, does it? That's how I felt when you two took the project from me." His tone was more reasoned than the two had seen the day before. He no longer had the ramblings of an insane man.

"I was gonna show them. My twenty-year reunion is next year. They used to tell me I was nobody, wouldn't amount to anything. I had it. I was gonna show them I was more successful than any of them. You took that away."

This is about more than just a bid, thought Jeff.

His voice was beginning to sound infuriated again.

We've got to calm him down, Gloria thought to herself.

"I'm sorry, Mike. I never thought it would come to this."

"You can come to work for me."

The offer was made to pacify Mike for the time being.

"Do you think I'm that stupid? I know I can't go to work for you now. The only place I would go after kidnapping you is to jail. I'm not stupid. I was smart enough to figure out that you paid Gloria to change my bid."

Jeff and Gloria exchanged a strange look.

"What was that look for?"

No answer.

Mike pulled Jeff out of the van and shoved him against a tree.

"I asked you a question, you piece of crap. What was that look for?"

A look of fear came over Jeff as Mike shoved his face into the tree with the pistol pushed sharply into his back.

"I didn't pay her anything. Didn't she tell you?"

"Tell me what?" He pushed the pistol harder into Jeff's back.

"Gloria and your boss were having an affair. I threatened to expose them if she didn't fix the bid."

A second of silence followed, as he recalled the memory of his confrontation with Tim when he tried to explain that Gloria had fixed the bid. Tim didn't listen to a word. He knew. The S.O.B. knew. He probably helped switch it to keep his dirty secret safe from his wife.

"Get the hell out of the van."

Gloria stepped out, uncertain if she should run or do what he asked.

"I'm sorry, Mike. I couldn't let my husband know. It would have killed him and the kids. PLEASE, MIKE. I HAVE KIDS," she pleaded.

"You miserable slut. You destroyed everything I worked for because you couldn't stay out of your boss's pants."

A surge of rage that had built up for the past two months suddenly gave in to all of its desires in light of the new revelations.

"YOU RUINED MY LIFE!"

Two shots fired into Gloria's chest. Her eyes looked at Mike as if to say, "I can't believe you just did that." Her mouth opened as she slowly fell to the ground.

"Damn you!" said Jeff, hoping to catch Mike off guard.

The words instead provided the warning he needed to defend himself against his oncoming assailant. Mike swiftly stepped to the side to avoid Jeff. Mike put his foot out, causing Jeff to fall to the ground with Mike standing over him from behind. Jeff knew instantly it would likely be the last mistake he would ever make. Smoke followed the bullet from the pistol that confirmed Jeff's final thought.

Jeff's body lay perfectly still on the ground.

"I killed them. Oh . . . no."

Mike's intention was to scare both of them. To make them realize what they had done. Now the reality of the situation hit him. He had killed them.

They took away my dream, he thought, trying to justify his actions.

A sudden terror that he would get caught came over him.

I can't face my classmates if they find out I did this.

He was suddenly filled with scenarios of what his life would be like after they found out he did it. He could feel the warmth of the gun and smell the fresh gunpowder as he put the pistol in his mouth and without emotion pulled the trigger.

CHAPTER 16

The sun's rays moved across the floor of the forest at various intervals determined by the passing clouds and the thick canopy of the large oak trees that reached towards the sky. The dramatic effect was only increased by the strange quietness that now filled the area.

Jeff stood in the largest of the sun's rays as it passed over him, watching Mike Hollister as he put the gun to his own temple.

What's he doing?

A minute of confusion passed over him as he tried to recall how he got here.

"No," he said, running towards Mike.

BOOM.

Oh, Mike, no.

He turned away from the horrible sight.

Can't believe I saw that and didn't lose my lunch.

He felt a wave of relief as it occurred to him he must have survived.

He must have missed me, he thought, recalling the shot. *But what about Gloria?*

Jeff turned to the spot where he saw Gloria fall. A growing pool of blood surrounded her in the dirt.

Oh, no.

Jeff looked away from the horrible sight, feeling a tug of responsibility for this mess.

No. It wasn't my fault. He pulled the trigger.

As he turned, he noticed a third body on the ground. Only one thought came to his mind as he recognized the third body.

I'm dead. He shot me, and I'm dead.

Jeff walked over to his body and tried to turn it over to look at his face.

I can't touch it. NO. I'm not ready to die. I've got more to do. What about all the things I was going to do when I sold my share of the company? I was going to travel and spend some time with my daughter I barely know. It can't be my time.

"It's time to go, Jeff."

"Robert? Is that you?" Jeff didn't know what else to say. He had envied his brother and resented the way everyone compared the way he ran the business, but now he was speechless upon seeing him.

"It's good to see ya, little bro."

"It was so hard without you. We were supposed to run the business together until we retired. You know, take our yearly fishing trip to Lake Latoon. I stopped taking that trip. Got too busy at work."

"Yeah, I'm afraid the business was too much for you. You would do anything to save that business. You almost gave up your soul for it, Jeff. You've done some bad things. Unnecessary things."

Try to defend what you've done, he thought, but deep down, seeing his dead body on the ground, knowing his life was over, he knew he had little defense. *None of the things I thought were important matter at all now.*

"Am I going to be able to stay with you?"

"You won't be able to stay with me now," answered Robert. "You have work to do. Come on."

A bright light appeared in front of them, and Robert stood up and walked in. Jeff gave one last glance at his unmoving body.

Guess this is it.

Jeff walked into the light and disappeared.

CHAPTER 17

The sky was filled with dark storm clouds, and the wind blew fiercely across the green pasture where Jeff now found himself. A large figure wearing a suit of armor and riding a massive black horse rode through the tall grass toward him, stopping close enough to Jeff that he could feel the hot breath of the Belgian whose lathered appearance said it had traveled a long way.

"Jeff McCarry. I have much to show you. Mount the horse and ride with me."

"What if I choose not to?" Jeff asked. The habit had been developed over his years as a businessman.

Find out why you should do something. What are the consequences if you do it or if you don't, and can you get something better? This was the philosophy he learned to live his life by.

"Then I suppose," stated the knight with a hint of a smile in his eyes, "as you watch me ride away from here in a few seconds you will be consumed by one thought: I wonder where he was going to take me?"

I don't know. Jeff's mind was racing. The businessman in him wanted to stay here and try to gain some advantage over this situation. *But what? What advantage is there?* he thought, trying to work this situation as though it were business.

"Have it your way." The knight turned his horse.

"Wait! I . . . I'll go."

Jeff was in awe at the feeling of power that came from riding on such a beast. The scenery flew by, giving him a sense of tremendous speed, yet the horse looked as though the run required little effort.

The knight pulled up to an area that didn't belong among the green pastures they had been riding through. A group of palm trees and white sand surrounded a pool of the clearest blue water Jeff had ever seen.

Even the weather seems different here.

The knight dismounted and made a motion indicating Jeff should do the same. Jeff dismounted, and the knight took the riding equipment off the horse.

"Go on, play."

The horse turned and ran as though he understood. The ground shook as the horse took off at a speed that more than doubled that which had brought them here.

"How come we didn't ride him here that fast?"

"Because I like to stay on the back of him when I want to get somewhere," the knight laughed.

"Jarod," he said, simply holding out his hand.

"Jeff McCarry."

Jeff took his first good look at the knight. His face was that of an old man, but his eyes were full of youth. There was energy in them that Jeff had never seen before.

Jarod looked at the small lake. The sun reflected onto his face, giving it a leathery texture. His beard was white minus a gray area just below his lips. His smile faded and a thoughtful expression crossed his face.

"What was J&R McCarry Company's greatest flaw this past year, Jeff?"

"That's easy. We couldn't get the projects done in time and had to pay liquidated damages, which ate up most of the profits we would have earned."

"What were you doing about it?"

"We were evaluating our production flaws. Man, machinery, and management. Top to bottom. We were making changes the way we always do when we come upon a problem."

"And the business's greatest strength?"

"We grew the company when we took over GH Logan, an up-and-coming firm. Our stock was worth roughly ten percent more with the addition."

Jarod paused for a second. "What about you? What was your greatest weakness this past year?"

"What do you mean?"

"You. What was your flaw that hindered you the most?"

Jeff tried to think of an answer, but nothing came to his mind.

"You kept such a close eye on the company, but you couldn't take the time to see what your own flaws were. Life is always changing, Jeff, and sometimes flaws work their way into our characters if we don't take time to look at ourselves and see what we're becoming."

"I . . ."

"How about greed, Jeff. Were you a little greedy this last year? Or maybe you were too willing to do anything to keep the company going, too willing to cheat and lie to get what you wanted, too busy stepping on people who were under you. Did you stop and look at yourself, Jeff? DID YOU?" Jarod's tone was harsh and quickening with each word.

The truth of the knight's words hit Jeff like knife.

"I . . . I didn't—"

"NO. YOU DIDN'T, DID YOU," the knight interrupted, cutting off whatever Jeff's words might have been. "YOU WERE TOO BUSY BEING AN ARROGANT, SELF-SERVING EXCUSE OF A MAN. YOU GOT MIKE AND GLORIA KILLED."

"NO . . . THAT'S NOT TRUE."

The thought that he was to blame for Mike and Gloria's death had crossed his mind, but to hear someone else say it was too much.

Jeff screamed as he flung himself at the knight.

The knight stood and dodged the oncoming attack. Jeff was caught by surprise that the old man could move so quickly. Jarod grabbed the back of Jeff's neck with one hand and pulled his right arm behind his back. Jeff struggled but could not overcome the old knight's strength.

"You need to take a look at yourself."

"Let me go or I'll—"

Jarod ignored whatever futile threat Jeff was about to make as he pulled him over to the edge of the water.

"LOOK!" he said, pushing Jeff's head into a position to allow him to see his reflection in the water.

"Let me go!" As Jeff strained to free himself, he caught his reflection in the pool. He ceased struggling.

Something strange about the reflection. It's looking at me. A chill ran through him.

Jarod released his grip and backed away.

I didn't move my eyes, but my reflection's eyes are moving.

"What . . . What do you want from me?"

His reflection slowly moved his hands from his side. Jeff's eyes widened in amazement.

Without warning, the reflection broke the surface of the water and met Jeff face to face. Jeff tried to back away, but the reflection, now as real as himself, grabbed him.

"Why don't you take a closer look, Jeff?" The reflection went quickly back under the surface, pulling his confused counterpart down with him.

CHAPTER 18

Jeff struggled against his reflection now pulling him down through the water with an alarming amount of force.

NO. It was the only thought that came to his panic-stricken mind.

He had swallowed a fair amount of water from the unexpected plunge, and despite the fear that overcame him he found it impossible to escape the grip of his reflection.

I'm going to die.

"You're not going to die. Well, at least not again, for a while, anyway," his counterpart said, smiling.

Jeff looked up to find himself sitting at the large oak table in the J&R McCarry conference room. He was surprised to see himself sitting at the side of the table instead of taking his usual place at the head.

Just forgot about it. It's a dumb idea. Jeff heard the thought in his mind, but knew it didn't belong to him. *I can't even make myself move. It's like someone else is in control, and all I can do is watch.*

"Well, where is our arrogant boss when you need him?" said a short slender woman with dark hair and glasses sitting across the table.

That's Kim Manchester, Jeff thought to himself.

"Be on time . . . I need your ideas," she continued with a sarcastic voice. "Hell, why doesn't he just tell us to come down here so he can shoot down our ideas and then tell us what we're going to do?"

She's talking about me.

"I thought you liked Jeff," replied a short, well-dressed man near the head of the table.

"It's called sucking up to the boss, Louie. I thought you of all people would recognize sucking up."

The group at the table seemed to enjoy the comment. The woman relished the attention she was getting at Jeff's expense and decided to continue.

"There's only one person that really likes him, Louie."

"Who, me?" mumbled Louie, trying cautiously not to become the butt of another joke.

"No, him."

I didn't have any idea they viewed me this way. I just wanted to keep the business running, and I tried to include them in these meetings so they would feel involved.

"What about you, Matt? You're the NEW guy. You got any NEW ideas?" said Kim, looking directly at Jeff.

Don't tell them what you're thinking. Jeff could hear the thought. *I'm Matt . . . Matt. What was his last name? He was supposed to be a financial genius. Thought maybe he would help pull our fat out of the fire. Never had any good ideas as far as I could tell. I don't think he stayed with us very long.*

Jeff McCarry burst into the room with a loud bang of the door. The room fell silent at his entrance.

"All right, people, we need to get some ideas to cure our financial situation. We've been in a slump, and right now I'm open to suggestions."

Wow. I've never sat back and took the time to listen to how I sounded. Where was the "Good morning . . . how is everyone today?"

Say it. It's a good idea.

What's this kid thinking? Jeff's curiosity was getting the better of him.

"I have an idea." Jeff could sense the nervousness Matt was feeling and the courage he had to find to even speak.

"What's your idea, Mike?" A wave of uneasiness swept through the room at the realization that Jeff got Matt's name wrong.

It's Matt, you jackass.

Sorry, Jeff thought in response to Matt's harsh thought.

Wow, that made him even more uncomfortable. Jeff could feel Matt's pulse quicken and his heart pounding as his blood pressure escalated.

"As best as I can figure Mr. McCarry, J&R Construction owns approximately $15 billion worth of equipment."

"That might be true," said Jeff with a look as though he wanted Matt to hurry up and spit out whatever it was he wanted to say.

"For the six months I've been here, at any given time there is about $8 billion worth of equipment just sitting in our yards gathering dust."

"Don't even think about selling it. We need that equipment for backup in case our other equipment breaks down."

"Why can't we just rent if that happens?"

"If we have it in our yards, we know we can use it and don't have to waste time trying to figure out where to rent it from."

"But we can—"

"NO. Now does anyone else have any ideas that will actually work?"

As Jeff heard himself say no he felt the disappointment Matt was feeling. He could also see the memory of Matt checking on the cost and availability of rental equipment.

That would have saved us money. He would have gotten the money from the sale of the equipment and we would have saved even more on property tax for the equipment we didn't use. This kid had it all worked out, and I wouldn't listen.

I need to find a company that can use me. Hell, I've got enough ideas on how to save this company money to put them well into the black if he could keep his arrogance out of the way.

The room disappeared before Jeff's eyes, and he was thrust into the center of a room surrounded on all sides by full-length mirrors.

Not my reflection again, thought Jeff, remembering the last glimpse of his reflection.

"Not pleasant to look at, is it?" Jarod asked.

Jeff turned to see one of his reflections that failed to mirror the image he was projecting, but was the old knight standing in front of him.

"I don't think I want to see any more of myself."

"It's not up to you, but you are done seeing the negative aspects of your life."

Jeff found himself sitting on the shore of the pond sitting on the bank line near the knight. Next to the knight stood a small girl he estimated to be about ten years old. Her eyes were shining, and a warm smile gave a sense that she was extremely happy.

The smile failed to penetrate the shame Jeff was now feeling in light of the scene he had just witnessed.

"I . . . I can't believe I paid that guy money to help us out financially and then I wouldn't take the time to listen. He would have kept the company from being in the distressed situation we were in, the situation which caused me to go to extreme measures to save it."

The memory of Gloria getting shot suddenly came back to him.

That's strange. I had put that out of my mind.

"Sometimes the little things we do or don't do end up being the major turning points in our lives. You might think you shouldn't have tried to blackmail Gloria, and you shouldn't have, mind you. But the situation would have not presented itself if you had taken the time and listened to Matt and he would still be happily employed at your company. That was the goal you and Robert started the company with," said Jarod.

"To provide a work environment that was supportive and didn't overlook anyone. That was our agreement after we left Carter Construction. They forgot about the employees and worried too much about the money. I lost sight of that. Robert never did. If I had stayed focused on them, they would have taken care of the company."

Jeff's head hung down. The shame of what he had become in his lifetime weighed upon him.

"I thought I was so great. I treated people like dirt. I want to make up for my life. What can I do to make up for the way I've treated people?"

"You'll get your chance, Jeff. If you desire it strongly, you will make up for every person you've wronged and every evil deed you justified as necessary. God has a plan for you," Jerod answered.

"What is that plan?"

"Jeff, I would like you to meet Susie." The knight ignored the question as he introduced the little girl who had stood by quietly as Jeff talked about the errors of his past.

"Susie, this is Jeff."

The girl's smile broadened as she stepped forward with her hand outstretched.

"Hello."

"Hi, Susie."

"He's going to take you to the light you see over there."

The knight pointed to the horizon at what Jeff had assumed to be some sort of astronomical entity such as a large sun setting behind a relatively large snowcapped mountain.

"I-I am?" Jeff stuttered, not too sure about the prospect of taking a kid across the wilderness and mountain he saw between him and the light.

"You asked what God's plan was for you. This is the beginning of it." Jarod grinned at the bewildered look on Jeff's face.

CHAPTER 19

The large Belgian ran toward the beckoning whistle of the old knight. The horse looked refreshed as though he had been rubbed down and cared for. Jeff grabbed the reins of the horse. His uneasy footsteps gave Jeff a sense that this animal did not like standing in place.

It must be like prison to him. To stand here when he could be running across these pastures. The freedom he must feel to move so swiftly and powerfully that very little can stop him.

"Come on, Susie," said Jeff, holding his hand down to pull her up with him. He swung her behind him, and she instantly put her arms around his waist. Jeff gave Jarod a look that gave way to the fact that in his life he had spent no time whatsoever with children and was unsure how to handle this situation.

"The horse will take you where you need to go. When the time comes, he will bring you back here. Susie won't be coming back." Jarod stepped aside to give the horse room.

"COME ON, BOY." Jeff dug his heels into the horse, causing him to take off at a high rate of speed. Jeff barely got a hold on the saddle horn as the horse ran towards a ray of light that looked to Jeff to be miles away across the green pasture. They passed trees, streams, and lakes more beautiful than any he had ever seen as they made the journey towards the light.

With no command from Jeff, the Belgian stopped near a stream. Full lush grass carpeted the ground in front of the large pine trees that fringed a rock-lined stream, in which flowed the cleanest water Jeff had ever seen. The grass swayed in the wind, giving an illusion of movement across the valley to the base of the mountain.

"Come on, boy." The horse would not move but turned his head to give him a look like he should be doing something besides sitting on his back.

"What? We're supposed to go to the light. We're close, but not there yet."

The horse made a nodding motion with his head.

"What? What do you want?"

"I think he wants us to get off him."

Jeff turned to look at Susie.

"Now why would he want us to do that?"

"He needs a break."

"Is that it, boy? You need a break?"

The horse shook his head again as though he understood.

Jeff climbed off the horse.

"All right, Susie, down you go," he said, reaching up to grab her.

As soon as her feet were on the ground, the horse took off across the pasture in the direction they had come from.

"NO!" Jeff cried out in disbelief as the horse disappeared into the heavy foliage at the opposite side of the open meadow.

"Now what do you suppose that was about?" Jeff said in an angry tone.

Jeff looked at Susie, hoping he didn't scare her.

"What are you laughing at?" he asked, seeing her trying not to laugh at the situation they now found themselves in.

"He just ran away," she said, laughing uncontrollably.

Jeff's first instinct was to be angry and try to figure this situation out from a logical standpoint. Now, he couldn't help but join in her laughter.

"All right, I guess it is funny then."

CHAPTER 20

Jeff and Susie sat on a large rock near the edge of the river. She had talked him into taking his shoes off and letting their feet soak in the cool stream.

"We don't have time for this," he insisted when she first suggested the idea to him.

"Where do we have to be?"

The question was so innocent and yet seemed so profound.

Even after I died I still can't get rid of my bad habits.

"Let's do it," he exclaimed, thinking it might be fun.

The breeze blew across his face as he and this child he barely knew sat in silence. In the distance he could hear the song of a bird he was not familiar with. He closed his eyes and took a deep breath.

"How did you die?" she asked, breaking the silence between them.

Jeff opened his eyes. He was hoping to hang on to the silence a little longer—enjoy the sounds and smell that came with this beautiful piece of heaven he was now in. Most of all he did not want to answer that question.

How could I ever tell anyone, most of all this innocent child, of the death I caused? Others and my own.

"It's okay. I understand about death. Even though I was young when I died, I'm as familiar with dying as you are. I don't remember much about my death . . . I think someone suffocated me."

Jeff gave a concerned look.

"I'm kind of the same way. I can't remember much about it. This place seems to take a lot of bad memories away." It was the truth. Had it not been for Jarod mentioning Gloria and Mike's names, he was almost certain he would have forgotten.

"I like it here," she remarked with a look of delight crossing her face.

"Me, too. I think this is one of the nicest places I've ever been."

Jeff sat back and closed his eyes to try to recapture the enjoyment he felt at the sounds filling this wonderful place.

CHAPTER 21

Susie sat on the large rock next to Jeff. His body lay motionless except for the rise and fall of his chest. He had drifted off to sleep listening to the sounds of the birds and the stream, and she decided it best to let him rest. She turned her head towards the mountain with one eye closed and the other closely inspecting two objects a distance from one another.

It is moving. She moved toward Jeff and nearly jumped on him in her excitement.

"It's moving towards us! It's coming! Wake up!"

"Wha-What is it?" It took him a second to regain his bearings.

"The light . . . it's coming to us!"

Jeff turned and looked up toward the mountain. The light they had seen in the distance was now much closer.

"Look at the size of it."

The light closely resembled a tornado only much larger and did not appear to be destroying anything. The base of the light was at the foot of the mountain, while the top matched the mountains in height.

"Look at how wide it is."

How come I'm not scared of it? Jeff thought to himself, baffled at how something that resembled a tornado would not make him want to run in terror.

"It's coming right at us!" Susie moved to the side to get a full view of the amazing sight.

"It's the greatest thing I've ever seen."

"I guess we wouldn't have time to get out of its way if we want—"

Jeff could not complete the sentence. He was no longer flesh and bone, but he felt almost breathless as the light moved on top of them.

It's so bright, but it doesn't hurt to look at it.

Where have I felt this before? It was so familiar, yet the memory escaped him.

"This is the union of souls, Jeff. Everyone's soul that has been on earth or will be on earth is here. We are all one in this union. You must join us and be consumed by the light so you can complete what you must do."

Jeff took a step forward and was thrust into a world of total awareness.

I was here before I was born. When I was waiting to become human.

Jeff was surrounded by other souls who spoke to him. There were many different souls, but they were all one. Now, Jeff was one with them.

You wasted life, Jeff. The thought was revealed to him, and it was the conscience of all of the souls combined in this perfect union.

So many souls, thought Jeff in awe of the sensations he was discovering.

But somehow only one soul.

Jeff could not tell which thoughts were his and which belonged to the union. His thoughts and memories were consumed by the one soul he was now a part of and he was at peace with a feeling that the soul was rejoicing for his return to it.

"I was taken out to live my life on earth. A life I was shown and accepted before I was born."

"We all accepted the lives we had on earth. Everything good and bad that happened in our lives was for the greater good. We all brought greater knowledge and through the struggles of our time on earth, a stronger soul back to the union we now share. This union that gives glory and praise to God. Now, Jeff, you must once again leave us to complete your life on earth."

Jeff said nothing but basked in the feeling of wholeness.

"Bye, Jeff."

Jeff saw Susie's bright eyes and warm smile as she peeked out of the light. Her face was glowing, and he understood what true happiness was as he watched her move toward the top of the union. Jeff felt himself separate from them. The bright light slowly moved away from him and he was left standing next to the horse in the open field.

Bye, Susie. Take care.

Jeff stood in amazement as he watched the union leave him behind.

CHAPTER 22

Jeff once again hopped onto the back of the black horse. He took off slowly not caring if the trip back took a long time. He had seen his reflection and returned to what he knew was home with the union. He wanted time to contemplate what he witnessed.

As the horse rode off, Jeff turned and looked back toward what was once again a light on the horizon, a part of him hungering to be reunited with the union and knowing deep within himself that they wished to have him and all of the souls back with them but for now they knew it was for the best. Those who were not with the group would someday return, while others would be dissected from the entity to spend their time on earth.

Seems strange that we forget the union. How can you forget something like that? I always wondered what that feeling of incompleteness I had was.

CHAPTER 23

Jeff dismounted and walked over to Jarod who was sitting, staring at the pool of water.

"You have questions, don't you?"

"Lots of questions."

"I will tell you everything I can, but some of your questions cannot be answered. You have a keen understanding of human nature. This quality will serve you well when you return to fulfill your duty, if you so choose. It's one of the reasons you were chosen. As well as it served you on earth fulfilling your own desires, it will now serve God's will. You know deep in your heart you're not meant to stay here. A voice inside you keeps telling you this. That voice is going to stay with you when you get back to earth."

The knight paused with a thoughtful look.

"Listen to that voice. When you start to stray from the path God wants you on, the voice will be harder to hear. If you do not hear the voice, it's time to ask yourself what you need to change about your life."

"Whose voice is it?"

"It is connected to the union, but it is yours. Your conscience, so to speak. You had that same voice when you were on earth, but you didn't listen to it. For many years the voice remained silent because you stopped listening. You were too concerned with building earthly wealth. When you are connected to the union, it will convey to you the will of God. Just because you're back on earth doesn't mean you can't listen to what heaven is telling you. You have a mission, Jeff. You feel you have to go back and complete it, despite the desire to stay with the union."

"I've felt it since I left the union. Something important."

"You have a lot to find out about your purpose on earth. You are going back to redeem sinners. You will be a keeper of the Holy Grail used in a ceremony that connects the sinner to heaven. It gives them their voice back. The voice tells them what is good and what is bad. Right from wrong and why it's better to choose good. It gives them a connection back to God's will in their life. It lets them know there is redemption and what they need to achieve it. The work you do will be important, but you must understand it is not your work, but the work of God you are doing. You will not see the world as you used to. No longer will you be concerned with possessions. You will have nothing, yet your life will never feel more complete."

Jeff began to feel a growing enthusiasm.

"You are dead, Jeff McCarry. Do you accept the work being assigned to you? You have the choice to decline, always. You will still have temptations you must overcome. The path that follows God's will is not an easy one, but it is the right one."

You want to do this. This is more important than anything you've ever done on earth before, his new voice was shouting at him.

"Yes, I accept."

"Then kneel and accept your fate."

Jeff knelt in front of Jarod. The old knight raised his sword.

"Do you understand you must die to your former self?"

"Yes."

"That to accept this position, great and honorable as it is, means to live humbly in the service of your fellow men?"

"I do."

"Then Jeff McCarry is no more. His existence is only a reminder of the failed attempts of some humans to achieve greatness, when that greatness is measured by earthly means. Die that which is Jeff McCarry and rise Larry Kincaid, servant of those who seek redemption."

The knight struck Jeff on the left shoulder with a solid blow from the flat side of his sword.

"Rise, Larry Kincaid, servant of God and servant of his fellow man." The sword struck his right shoulder with a solid blow.

"Rise, Larry Kincaid. Where once was Jeff McCarry, an arrogant man serving only himself, rise Larry Kincaid and serve a cause much greater than yourself." The sword fell on top of his head. Blackness surrounded his vision, starting from the outside edges and working swiftly inward.

CHAPTER 24

The three bodies lay still, face down on the forest floor. Each one faced away from the others, forming a triangle between them. Gloria's long blond hair moved slightly as a small breeze blew across it. Her open eyes held a glazed appearance that left no doubt she was lifeless.

Mike laid face down nearly twenty feet away. The side of his head that lay upward was mangled from the exit wound of the bullet.

The area held an eerie silence. No birds were singing; all the animals had vacated the area after the sound of gunshots filled the air.

Jeff McCarry's body lay lifeless on his stomach. His face turned sideways to allow a full view of it. The wound on the back of his head left no doubt it was fatal.

His eyes suddenly lost the glazed appearance, and his body flinched. The wound on the back of his head healed, leaving no scar behind. His eyes blinked and turned a lighter shade of blue. He stood and looked around. A second of pain overcame him as his wound finished healing. He reached up and felt it. The memory of dying came to him as the wound continued to heal.

"Larry Kincaid. I'm Larry Kincaid."

His hands began to tingle.

"I'm changing."

He ran to the van to look at himself in the mirror.

I don't even look like Jeff McCarry.

His face was not drastically changed, but he would never be recognized by anyone he ever knew. His hair turned slightly gray as though he had aged nearly ten years.

Even my eyes are a different tone. Brighter, full of life. I'm not Jeff McCarry. The thought came to him as though it were the most natural of things.

Gloria? Mike?

A wave of extreme guilt overtook him.

"OH, NO. What have I done?" His knees gave out from under him.

Slowly he stood back up and walked to Mike's body and knelt beside him.

"I'm so sorry," he gasped.

A sense that this gruesome scene served a higher purpose came over him.

"I trust You, God, that this is serving a purpose I, in my human ignorance, cannot fathom. Please forgive my contribution to their suffering."

Larry leaned down to look at Gloria's lifeless face.

I wish I could ask your forgiveness, Gloria. I'm sorry I used your past against you. I will call the authorities to get your bodies. From there they would figure out that Mike had murdered you and turned the gun on himself.

They, however, would never know he was at the scene.

"Go fulfill your mission." He could hear the voice. It seemed so right and so easy when he was talking to Jarod about redeeming sinners, but now that he was back in the flesh he was struck with extreme feelings of doubt and fear.

"Oh, God, why me? I'm such a sinner. How can I help other people when I can't even take care of myself?"

CHAPTER 25

Larry walked into the adobe-style house considered average in this small town of Larendo, Mexico. He waved at the man in the blue Chevy as it took off.

"Thanks, Juan."

A short black man dressed in colorful clothing greeted Larry at the door.

"Ahh. Larry Kincaid, I assume," he said pulling his hand from underneath the robed clothing and offering it to Larry. "Keither Lal."

"Pleasure to meet you," replied Larry, shaking his hand.

"Come, there are others who are excited to meet you." Keither smiled as he turned towards the only other door into the room they were standing in.

Larry followed Keither into a small dining room with a table that looked to have been made from whatever wooden material was lying around outside the house.

"Gentlemen and Nikita, I would like you to meet Larry Kincaid."

Four men sitting around the table stood up as though they had been introduced to some famous dignitary. A young Chinese man took the liberty of introducing himself first. "Yen Pong. It is an honor to meet you, Mr. Kincaid," he said, bowing slightly.

The introductions took off as though they had been rehearsed.

"Fenton Green. I'm from Germany." Fenton gave an amazed look as he shook Larry's hand. "It is an honor to meet you." His green eyes glowed as though he were a child waking up on Christmas morning to a stack of presents under the tree.

"Nikita Merkovi." The tall blond woman took Larry's hand. Her smile and bright blue eyes captivated Larry for an instant.

"Um . . . pleasure to meet you, Nikita," replied Larry.

"Pleasure's all mine," she returned in a voice that sounded like she enjoyed watching Larry stumble over his words.

"Well, now that the introductions are over, I'm sure Larry has some questions he would like to have answered." Keither looked at Larry as if to say, you do have questions, right?

Larry gave a nod.

"We have all been chosen to serve a purpose higher than ourselves. We bring redemption to the sinner. We would not have the power to do this if it were not given to us from above. We must always keep in mind that we are servants no matter the greatness of our work."

"Are you familiar with the Holy Grail, Mr. Kincaid?" Yen took advantage of Keither's pause to hasten the explanation.

"You mean the cup used at the last supper?"

"Yes."

"I've heard of it."

"We hold it in our possession. The five of us are responsible for maintaining possession of the grail and its proper use for the redemption of sinners. It holds amazing power, Mr. Kincaid." Yen's eyes glowed passionately as he talked about the grail.

Everyone in the room looks like they're on a high talking about the grail.

"What do we do with the grail?" Larry asked, trying to encourage one of them to start speaking again.

"We represent the five continents," Yen said, taking the opportunity to pick up where he left off. "That gives us each two months and some change that the grail is in our care. By taking it to the people who need redemption and having them drink from it, we fulfill our duty until it is time for someone to take our place."

"Then what?"

"Then we will go on to complete whatever task God has chosen for us, whether it be a small task or the one God has for you when you complete your time as grail keeper."

"What task is that?"

Yen and the others smiled.

"That will be revealed to you by God in his time," Keither replied.

"I assume I am responsible for North America when my two months come around."

"You are correct." Nikita spoke for the first time since the introductions.

"How will I communicate when I'm in the non-English speaking areas of the continent?"

Fenton smiled. "You don't think all of us here know how to speak English, do you?"

The room fell silent to give Larry a moment to comprehend the recent information he had just been given. "But . . . " He wanted to ask how, but his mind had stopped as it tried to process the new information.

"Same concept as speaking in tongues," Yen jumped in, always excited to be the one to explain how the system worked. "We all speak in our native languages, but here we all understand each other. I assume you met some people on your trip here who you were thrilled to learn spoke English."

"You mean . . ." It had not occurred to Larry that he had met a fair amount of people who spoke English so far south of the border.

"Not everyone will be able to understand you. If you are in a room with two people, one who speaks English and the other Spanish, you will only be able to communicate with the one who speaks your language so no one outside of our group realizes the miracle that is taking place."

Larry looked around the room at the different nationalities gathered.

"Hard to comprehend," said Fenton. "We all experienced the union through our near-death experiences and we are almost certain that experience is what gave us those gifts. We also receive the power to see what our mission is, but this gift does not come to us until we drink from the grail."

"Are you ready to drink from the grail, Larry Kincaid?" The question came from Keither, whom Larry had originally assumed was leader of the group but now realized all held an equal place.

"I'm ready."

Nikita reached down and grabbed a briefcase. She opened it up. Inside was a wooden cup.

"Is that the grail?"

"Yes." Fenton took the glass pitcher on the table and poured water into the grail. "May you do all God asks of you with an unquestioning enthusiasm that he will find pleasing."

Nikita handed the cup to Larry. Larry took the cup and looked around the room at the others who had drank from this cup.

"To unquestioning enthusiasm." Larry put the cup to his lips and drank.

CHAPTER 26

The sun was shining on the city of Peking, China. Larry stood on the side of a hill looking down on the large city. He took a deep breath as the wind blew across his face.

"Have you ever been to China?"

Larry turned, surprised to see a young man in a white three-piece suit standing behind him.

"I'm Marty," said the young man as an innocent smile crossed his face.

"Uh . . . um . . . Larry Kincaid. How did you get here?" Larry was sure he would have heard him come up behind him.

"How did you get here?" he returned.

"Well, I'm not sure." Larry blinked, trying to recall how he had come to this spot in China when his last memory was falling asleep at the house in Mexico.

"I'm dreaming. That's it," said Larry at the sudden revelation.

"You could call it that. I've been sent here to show you where you are going and things you need to do. You will only be told and shown what you need to do to complete the task God has chosen for you."

"Are you . . . " Larry hesitated not exactly sure what he wanted to ask.

"I'm an angel. A messenger doing the work of God. Yen will be taking the grail to Asia when everyone leaves Mexico. You are to go with him and see the sinners redeemed. First I want to introduce you to someone."

A strange sensation ran through Larry's body. Almost instantly he found himself standing in a small apartment filled with loud music and Chinese teenagers.

"The girl in the green shirt at the table is Lynn Won. Lynn's parents are out of town for the weekend, and she decided to have a party."

Larry spotted Lynn sitting almost directly across the table from where he and Marty were standing.

"I'm partying all night!" she screamed with a wild look in her eyes.

The table was surrounded with kids watching the excitement she seemed to be the center of.

"Take a look in her eyes, Larry."

Larry walked over closer to her and bent down to see her eyes. They were wide open, but it looked to Larry like she was ready to burst open.

"She's higher than a kite."

"Take a closer look. Can you see what she sees?"

Larry bent over once again and looked directly into them.

"What is that? I . . . " Larry couldn't put to words what he saw in her eyes. He then saw the opposite side of the room.

"What the—"

Larry no longer saw Marty. He was sitting at the table with two lines of cocaine in front of him.

I'm so wasted. The thought was not his.

I'm in her body . . . or her mind.

Larry saw many memories of her doing drugs. It started out so small.

Can quit anytime I want.

Now reason and sanity no longer existed in this mind. The addiction was all there was.

The drugs. Where and when can I get them and use them?

"She's out of control," Larry said, suddenly finding himself standing next to Marty, watching the chaos from a bystander's view.

"That's not all, Larry. See the guy going into the bedroom? Lynn's little sister is in that room. She cried herself to sleep about thirty minutes ago when Lynn yelled at her because she wanted Lynn to put her to bed."

A feeling of rage surged through Larry. "We have to stop him."

"You're watching something that happened almost two years ago, Larry. Lynn went into the room the next morning and found the guy passed out on top of her. She was dead. The man had tried to stop her screams but ended up suffocating her. He didn't even know he killed her until the next morning."

Larry's feeling of rage turned to a feeling of sickness.

"Lynn is unable to forgive herself. If she doesn't find a way, she will be driven to insanity."

"She's to blame for this, too. Him and her are both to blame."

"And what about Gloria and Mike? Do we not allow the person involved in their death forgiveness?"

"I . . . I'm sorry. I know people would be just as disgusted at me as I am about this. It's hard not to want to judge the situation. When I died and was shown some of the things I would do, it seemed so easy to accept the things God wants of me. Now that I'm back in a human body I still do things I shouldn't and I don't feel like I can do what God is asking me. I . . . I just feel incapable or unworthy. What gifts or talents or whatever you want to call it do I have that will do this girl any good? I've never been one to help others."

"Don't be too hard on yourself, Larry. It would be easy if you didn't have to live as a man. That's why God created the flesh so the spirit would be challenged and be capable of becoming stronger."

It makes me feel weak. Like I can't do it. I guess if I make myself do what they ask it will make me stronger. Larry glanced up at Lynn. *She is a lot like I was—just doing what she wants and not aware of the damage it's causing. Hope I can help you, Lynn. Neither one of us did the horrible deeds, but the bad things we did had a direct effect on the situation.*

"How can I help her, Marty?"

"That's the man God needs for you to be, Larry. Compassionate, not judgmental. You've experienced things that will help you understand the people you will be helping. You will be going with Yen to China to help her."

CHAPTER 27

The bedroom at the most southeasterly corner of the adobe house was filled with eerie shadows from the near full moon shining through the room's only window. Four silhouettes could be seen sleeping on the cots neatly placed to allow for a walkway near the center of the room. The four men had taken the larger bedroom and left the smaller for Nikita to allow her privacy.

Larry awoke from his dream and glanced up at the moon. He got up from his cot as quietly as possible and made his way into the small bathroom situated between the two rooms. He closed the door quietly and turned to the basin to wash the "old" feeling from his face.

"Larry Kincaid," he said to himself as he caught his reflection in the small wood-framed mirror that was hung so low he remained hunched over to see his reflection. Slowly he wiped the thick dust from the mirror.

I guess if we ever find that McCarry guy, we'll give him a piece of our mind about the incident in the forest.

"Do you still see your old self in there, Mr. Kincaid?"

Larry turned, startled at the feminine voice with the slight Russian accent when he thought no one else was around.

"I don't know. I see a physically different man than who I was and a lot of me has changed inside also. I want to be better, to do better."

"Let's talk outside so we don't wake the others."

Larry followed Nikita out the front door and into the sparsely grassed yard. The moon was almost directly above them and was full enough that about half the stars were not visible.

"Looks like a good night for a walk, Mr. Kincaid."

"Call me Larry."

"Why do you suppose, Larry, that our physical appearances were changed when we had our experiences?"

Larry hesitated for a moment. He had thought of several reasons for this, but some of the reasons he came up with would sound foolish to speak out loud.

"I . . . well . . . maybe so we don't have to look at ourselves in the mirror in disgust for some of the things we've done in the past." Larry gave her a quick glance to see her reaction. A slight look of his explanation being a possibility crossed her face.

He asked, "Why do you think our appearance changed?"

She paused for a second to find the right words. "Because we changed. Inside and out. We had to change to complete the work God wants us to do. The minute we accepted our work we changed inside. You and me, we gave up the person we used to be. We had to become somebody new because the old us ceased to exist. Not looking the part might help us to believe the old us doesn't exist. The same way a seed turns into a plant and is no longer the seed." A look of satisfaction crossed her face. She had communicated exactly what she was feeling.

"That makes sense to me," he said, raising an eyebrow.

"When I look in the mirror now," she continued, "I don't see my old self or even my new self. I see what I can become. The potential I have to do what God wants. It gives me the ability to do what he wants me to and the ability to forgive myself."

"What's your theory on the new names? I can't for the life of me figure out the names. I mean, take Larry Kincaid for example. That doesn't strike me as extremely religious or even meaningful. Why wouldn't I have been given a name from the Bible, say Peter or even Joshua. That would make more sense."

"Are you familiar with the story of Saul on the road to Damascus?" Nikita asked, turning to Larry.

"Vaguely."

"I wonder if when his name was changed to Paul if he thought it should have been Moses or Abraham. Might have made him feel as though expectations of him were incredibly high or that he needed to do the same things they did. Maybe God didn't want him to feel like that. Wanted him to feel like his mission in life was unique and naming him after someone else would take that away."

"That sounds reasonable, Nikita. His experience does sound a lot like ours. I wonder if he had a near-death experience. He may have belonged to the Order."

"Maybe," replied Nikita.

The rest of the walk remained quiet.

CHAPTER 28

The workers slowly made their way into the large metal building that housed a four-star auto parts business in Mankata, Washington. Their silence was the familiar ceremony of the factory workers mentally preparing themselves for the next eight monotonous hours. The job provided them with the money to pay the bills, insurance, and a bond with fellow workers that empowered them to make it through the injustices of the workplace and the trials that came from other areas of their life. As much as they appeared to dread the start of the work day, this factory provided them with the means to raise their children, put them through college, take care of them during any financial, health, or family crisis that would present itself to them, and eight hours of social interaction with people who became as close as family.

"Ready to make some brake pads."

Kirk smiled at the petite blonde that made the blue coveralls and safety glasses each worker was required to wear look attractive. He had worked with Stephanie for two years and enjoyed the enthusiasm she displayed that made him believe she liked coming to work here.

"You know it, Stephanie. But I don't like it near as much as you do."

"Do ya wanna go for that beer yet?" Stephanie would ask Kirk almost daily.

Kirk worked with Stephanie since his first day on the job. She was a nice-looking woman, who worked hard at the factory and just wanted to have a little fun after work. She would often talk about where her and her friends had gone the night before or what club they went to over the weekend. Kirk found her attractive and enjoyed her cheerful conversation at work but had no interest in dating at this point. However hard she tried to break down the wall he had built around himself, he worked twice as hard to maintain it.

"No, thanks," would be his only reply.

"Sometime maybe I can show you how to have a little fun," she would say with a smile that tried to hide the disappointment of being turned down.

Stephanie was nearing her thirties. Though she was a beautiful woman, throughout her high school years she never felt attractive. Time had taught her that with her natural looks and the right amount of confidence she could convince men she was worth a look. She developed a soft spot for Kirk. He knew she just wanted to have fun, and she never drove when she drank, but he had not touched alcohol or another woman since the night of Sarah's death. He just couldn't allow himself to get close to either one.

Any man at this factory would jump at the invitation she gives me almost every day. Kirk always compared his lack of interest in dating her to the way the mind made one lose their taste for a certain food after that food has made them vomit.

He never spoke to anyone about the night of the wreck anymore. At first he tried to speak to some friends about it, but he could tell from their reaction they didn't understand. They tried, with good intentions, to offer advice, but he just wanted someone to talk to that understood his misery.

At least the people out here in Washington don't have a clue who I really am. Not that it matters much because I still do and I can't get away from me.

His family had been good to him through his ordeal. They stuck with him no matter how wrong he had been or how much damage he had done, but even they failed to understand what he was going through. This would be his fourth job since high school. Losing Sarah had turned his life upside down. He had trouble focusing on work. The guilt he felt was unbearable. It had been seven years since he had taken Sarah's life. This was the way he looked at it. The way people treated him confirmed the guilt he felt in his heart. He wondered if they thought that would make him sorry for what he had done. He didn't know how he could be any sorrier than he already was.

Kirk remembered the wreck and the years following. It was like dropping a giant nuclear bomb. He would think about the people he had hurt by killing Sarah: Sarah's parents, grandparents, sisters, brother, friends, and himself—everyone that knew and loved her, he had hurt. Worse than he ever hurt anyone before he hurt all these people. Every dream Sarah and he had, he had taken away. Everything she was or was going to be was gone because of one night of carelessness.

Kirk tried to put it out of his mind, but when it did creep back in, the waves of guilt would be almost unbearable. He had vowed from that day forth to change. He would try his best not to harm other people. He changed his ways, but it did not seem to matter to anyone who knew him.

He was "the killer" to many of the people in his hometown. No matter how much good he had done in his life before this, or how much he would do, this one moment defined him to the people of his hometown. He was unforgiven by others and by himself.

I've hurt people in my life but never to a point that "I'm sorry" wouldn't take care of the hurt. That thought was unbearable to him.

The probation time he had to serve for his manslaughter charge due to his adolescent status was easy. *Death would be better than living with this persistent guilt,* he decided as he fantasized about ways to end it. *Dad's old shot gun,* he thought. He imagined the cold metal passing through his lips, accidentally scraping his teeth with the barrel. The thoughts seemed real; he smelled the old gunpowder that lightly coated the inside of the barrel as he took one last breath in.

Keep it pointed back.

Kirk heard of people not pointing it far enough back and living through it.

Lots of plastic surgery.

I've got to stop thinking like this.

As the days wore on, Kirk entertained the notion of suicide more often. Thinking of ways to release himself from this nightmare of solitude became an obsession. His family tried to reach out to him, but he became withdrawn. Kirk realized the growing insanity that was his mind.

Oh, my God. I'm losing it.

The sobs came uncontrollably. He had never cried so long or so hard in all his life. After what seemed like hours of sobbing, he was exhausted. With the outpouring of emotion came a new resolve to maintain his sanity. He forced himself to finish high school.

"It's important," his mom would tell him.

Nothing felt important at the time. He suffered his way through high school. Finishing the high school work was not the problem, but seeing the people he hurt daily was torture. This town was too small to avoid it. He could not make eye contact with the people in this town. So many people loved Sarah, and he had taken her away. They said nothing to him, but it showed in the way they looked away as they passed him. The stares they gave across the room. The whispering when they thought he couldn't hear.

He left Lansing the day he graduated. The few times he returned, he visited his family but gave no forewarning to his arrival. Five years had passed, and all the counseling and therapy he had gone through had little effect. He thought of turning to drinking but considering it was the problem to begin with he stayed clear of it.

That would be the end of what little chance I have to be perceived as a good human being by the people back home.

CHAPTER 29

Kirk stepped out of his apartment building into the pouring rain. The rain had continued for the past four days and showed no sign of ending.

It was Sunday morning, and he was on his way to church. Out of habit from his childhood he rarely missed going to church. His parents were devout Catholics who only missed Sunday Mass in extreme situations.

Better take the car, even though it's just a few blocks. I'd be soaked by the time I got there in this downpour.

Kirk jumped into the car. Through the rain he noticed a figure standing in front of the apartment buildings across the street.

Is he looking at me?

He rolled down his window to allow for a better view. Kirk partially closed his left eye as he struggled to see into the rain that was blowing into his window. The well-dressed man smiled at Kirk from under his black umbrella.

Strange!

The man waved at Kirk and with a grin turned and walked down the street.

If he didn't have that umbrella, I would say he doesn't realize it's raining so hard. Sure are some crazy people around here. Better hurry—five minutes and I'm gonna be late.

His parents always made sure to arrive at church with a good twenty minutes to spare. A habit he had broken from his childhood. *I know I'm not that late. There's usually a flood of people this close to Mass time. The rain must have kept a lot of them home, I guess.*

Kirk quickly walked up the stairs into the church, trying to stay as dry as he could, still surprised at the lack of people coming into the church. The church was empty except for two older women standing near the front engaged in some conversation that had them both excited enough to talk at the same time.

I know it's Sunday. How come no one's here?

"Did ye forget to spring forward, lad?"

Kirk turned to see a short balding man with a thick Irish accent coming out of the small room at the rear of the church.

"What's that, Father?" replied Kirk half startled.

"Daylight savings time. Ye were supposed to set your clock forward one hour last night," answered the priest, smiling at the confused look on Kirk's face.

"Oh, that's right. That explains why there's no one here."

"Saint Peter's has a 12:00 Mass on the other side of town," said the priest, "if yer interested."

"Thanks, Father," replied Kirk who had already decided on staying here for a quick prayer and then heading back to his apartment to watch the game at noon.

Kirk walked towards the front of the large church. He was surprised how his footsteps echoed in church with no one else here. He was rarely in church other than Sundays when the church was full of people.

"Ye should sit that close to the front during Mass, lad," said Father William with a smile as he headed into the sacristy.

Kirk smiled. He did usually have a tendency to take a seat towards the back of the church during the Mass. Now with no one here it seemed fitting to take a seat towards the front.

Kirk knelt down and let the silence of the church relax him. As he prayed, thoughts of Sarah and feelings of guilt began to take over.

This had become a way of life for him. The guilt would come with no warning, especially in moments of silence. Tears came as he replayed the events of the night Sarah died.

Where am I? Kirk looked down the embankment to see his truck on its top with steam rolling up from the front end.

"SARAH!"

Kirk stumbled down the hill, falling into the truck as the momentum carried him down the steep incline faster than his wounded body could control.

"Sarah?"

Kirk was certain when he first saw her bloody face and closed eyes as she lay on the interior side of the roof that she was dead.

"Oh, Sarah."

Sarah's eyes snapped open and a look of intense pain crossed her face.

"Oh, Kirk, it hurts," she moaned.

"Hold on . . . I'll go get help. Just hold on."

"You suppose it will ever quit raining?" asked a voice interrupting Kirk's thought.

Kirk turned startled to see the man that had been standing across the street from his apartment earlier that morning.

"Do I know you?"

"No, you don't, and I don't know you, but I've been sent here to help you get rid of your guilt."

How does he know about the guilt?

Up close the man looked a little older than Kirk had previously estimated. His suit, despite being out in the rain, appeared to be neatly pressed with nothing out of place. He held his hat in his hand in a way that made Kirk assume was out of respect for being in a church. His glasses gave him a look of intelligence.

"There is an organization of people who have suffered from the same type of guilt that has haunted you. It's an order so secret that few people know it exists and even they are uncertain of how large the organization is."

"What does this organization do?"

"Redeems the sinner. Removes the guilt that has stained their soul for too long. It's a second chance," exclaimed the man with a sudden glow in his eye.

The man stood, reached into his pocket, and pulled out a business card.

"Think about it," he said, handing the card to Kirk. "You've learned to live with the guilt, now you need to decide if you want to live without it. It's time to defeat your dragon."

The man turned and walked away.

"But how . . ."

The man kept walking as though he didn't hear him. Kirk looked at the card. "The Order of the Redeemed" was in large gothic-looking letters. Underneath in smaller text was an address: 564 High View Road, Indemnity, South Dakota.

CHAPTER 30

Lynn sat on the edge of the mattress in the small bedroom of the Orders house in Walong, China. She had just checked the hallway to make sure no one was stirring about.

This is such a pathetic ritual, she thought as she pulled a worn-out picture of her little sister out of her purse. Tears instantly began running down her face.

"I'm so sorry," she sobbed. "I . . ." She swallowed hard. "I didn't know it would happen."

I hope this redeemed stuff works, she thought, trying to control her sobbing that was growing louder.

A knock on the door caused her heart to jump.

"Who's there?" she mumbled, wiping the tears from her cheeks.

"Lynn, my name is Larry Kincaid. I'm with the Order. I would like to talk to you if you have a minute."

I don't usually let strangers into my room, but then again, I don't usually take trips to strange places like this. After all, doing the stuff I normally do hasn't gotten me anywhere.

"Come in," she replied, opening the door for him. "Lynn Won."

Larry shook her outstretched hand. "Larry Kincaid. Nice to meet you, Lynn."

He paused for a second uncertain what to say to get the conversation in a direction that might help Lynn comprehend she wasn't alone and that some people would truly understand her.

Help me out here, God. I don't even know what to say, he thought as a feeling of certain failure of his mission overtook him. *Why did you send me? There has to be someone better.*

"How was your trip here?"

"It was fine," she replied. "Traveled about one hundred and twenty miles to get here."

"I had a vision of what happened that night, Lynn."

She folded her hands and bowed her head slightly.

"No. No. I didn't mean to embarrass you. I just want you to know I understand how that can happen. Once upon a time, I let myself get out of control with power, and people died because of some of the decisions I made. But you have to realize when you chose to do the drugs you didn't make a malicious decision for your sister to die. I saw the man who went in that room. It was him that killed her."

"BUT I LET HIM IN THE HOUSE!"

"Easy, Lynn. You don't have to be so eager to convict yourself. You didn't have a . . ." Larry noticed a picture of a young black-haired girl sitting on the bed next to Lynn's purse. Goosebumps instantly formed on his arms, and a chill ran through him.

"Is everything alright?"

"This is Susie," he stated in a manner that made Lynn wonder if he was asking or telling her.

"Yes, that's Susie."

"She's your sister."

"Yes."

"Lynn, I'm going to have to ask you to sit down while I tell you a story about your Susie."

"You know her?"

Larry shook his head.

"I used to be a businessman. Let's just say I could have done better with my business practices and leave it at that. To make a long story short I ended up face down with a bullet in the back of my head. I was dead. Have you ever heard of a near-death experience?"

Lynn nodded.

"I was taken to a beautiful place where I was shown my faults and some of the things I should do to redeem myself. Lynn, I met Susie in heaven."

Lynn's head remained tilted to the floor as her brown eyes looked upward to examine his face, searching for any expression that would give his story credibility.

"She was happy. I was told to take her to a light a long distance away from us at the time. We rode a horse past trees and streams. It was the most beautiful place I had ever seen."

Lynn listened intently as he told her about the union of souls he had taken Susie to.

"I'm so happy to hear she's in that place." She jumped off the bed and gave Larry a hug, feeling a connection to her sister through him. "Thank you. Thank you," she sobbed.

"It was my pleasure. She's a fine girl," he replied, breaking the hug so he could look at her.

"She was a special person. After spending a little time with her I see why God wanted her back with him."

Lynn smiled at the comment as she wiped the tears off her face.

Larry turned and walked toward the door. "Oh. By the way, she didn't remember any of the details about her death."

A sense of relief came over Lynn at the thought of Susie forgetting the last horrific moments of her life. Larry closed the door, leaving her with a smile that would last longer than any she had had for the past two and a half years.

CHAPTER 31

Kirk sat at the small table in the corner of his kitchen flipping the business card across the fingers of his left hand.

This can't be right. But how did he know? Who was he?

He wanted to believe he could live like he did before the accident. He had come to envy people who had never allowed themselves to stumble and cause themselves guilt.

What if I could go through one day and not think about it? One day. Just go to my usual day of work or enjoy my time off with no thought of the accident or the people I hurt. Sarah, would it be okay if I didn't think about you for a little while?

What if I do let go? Does that mean I don't love you anymore, Sarah, or that I just forgot about you? I can't just give up the way I feel about you . . . I mean, felt about you.

Man, I don't even know if I'm talking to me or Sarah. I guess she's not alive anymore. I need to stop trying to talk to her.

And what about the people I hurt? Don't they deserve for me to feel guilty about what I've done? Isn't it an injustice for them if I move on?

They don't have any intention of forgiving me. Do I deserve their forgiveness? Hell, do I deserve forgiveness from myself?

Maybe I'll never get their forgiveness, but at least I can try to forgive myself.

The factory he worked for had a policy of one week's notice for taking vacation, so Kirk still had a week to decide before he was able to leave Washington. By the week's end, he had decided to take the trip.

Five days of vacation, so I'll have to be back by Monday.

Friday, after work, he loaded up his small car with the provisions he felt he would need to make the twenty-hour trip. As the miles passed, Kirk's mind was racing. His thoughts went from being redeemed, to the certainty there was nothing in South Dakota but a hoax. This idea had been in the back of his mind but did not come to the front until he crossed the Washington–Idaho state line.

There may not even be anything at this address. What if it's someone's house who doesn't know what the heck I'm talking about? I'm just going to fill up with gas at this convenience store and turn around and head back for home.

I can show up at work on Monday and save my vacation for later. This is one of the dumbest things I've ever done.

I guess sometimes when you want something bad enough you don't question it fully.

Kirk pulled around the gas station after filling up and grabbing a cup of coffee. At the exit to the gas station stood a large man holding a sign Kirk was certain would say, "Will work for food." Kirk reached into his wallet to pull out a dollar. He had trouble sleeping when he went by these guys without giving them something.

Kirk's eyes met the nervous-looking man's wide green eyes. He gave the man an uncertain smile as he rolled down the window. Kirk's heart skipped a beat. On the sign he was holding in large green letters written in crayon were the words Indemnity, South Dakota.

This has to be more than a coincidence.

I don't pick up hitchhikers . . . usually . . . but usually I don't take trips to South Dakota on a whisper of hope.

"Hop in," muttered Kirk with an uncertain tone.

Try to at least sound a little intimidating. If he is thinking about mugging you, the lack of confidence you just had in your voice just told him he should.

"Thanks."

The man sat down in the seat and struggled to tilt his head forward enough to fit the rest of him in the car.

"Ron Truitt," said the stranger, sticking his hand out to shake.

"Kirk Murphy. Nice to meet you."

He looks a little friendlier up close. I think it's his size that makes him appear threatening.

"Where are you from?" asked Ron as they turned out of the gas station towards South Dakota.

"Mankata, Washington. How about you?"

"Right here in Binesford, Idaho," replied Ron with a puzzled look.

"Did I say something wrong?" he asked catching the look on his face.

"I just thought you might know that."

"How would I know where you are from since I just met you?"

"Your friend I met yesterday seemed to know a lot about me. I thought he might have told you."

This conversation is getting us nowhere, thought Kirk.

"What friend are you talking about?" asked Kirk, trying not to sound as frustrated as he felt.

"Yesterday a man woke me up, took me into his hotel room for a shower and breakfast, and told me I should stand at that gas station with that sign and you would pick me up and take me to where I should go."

"He said I would pick you up?"

"He said someone in a yellow Chevy Lumina would pick me up. You were the only one I saw and you stopped like you knew to pick me up. You need to take me back to that gas station if you're not the one taking me to Indemnity," insisted Ron, almost sounding frantic at the thought of being in the wrong car.

Kirk was becoming a little concerned at his reaction. He couldn't remember the last time he had seen someone get excited so easily.

"Now settle down," said Kirk calmly. "I think you're in the right car. I was on my way to Indemnity and decided to turn around and go back to

Mankata after I filled up with gas. When I saw your sign I felt that was an indication I needed to keep going to Indemnity, so I picked you up."

Kirk and Ron exchanged disbelieving glances at the circumstances that had brought them to this point.

"I think someone wants us both in Indemnity," said Ron.

"Another strange point to this story," added Kirk, "I was the only one besides the man I met in the church who knew where I was going and he didn't know what time I was leaving."

For the rest of the trip, Kirk and Ron kept discussing the possibility of why they were heading to South Dakota. Ron shared with Kirk his story about the cocaine habit that distanced him from his wife and kids and tore his family apart.

"I kicked the habit, but not until after my wife ran away with the kids. I haven't seen them for nearly five years. I just can't seem to let go of the guilt," said Ron, forcing back the lump in his throat. "My only consolation is the kids were better off without me at that time. I sure would like one more chance."

"Maybe that's what we're gonna get in South Dakota," replied Kirk excitedly. "I mean, think about it. We're both on our way to a place where they told us we could be redeemed, and we both have guilt and are unable to make things right for the people we hurt."

The car remained silent for almost an hour as both men tried to grasp the circumstances that brought them on this strange journey.

CHAPTER 32

Kirk pulled into the small town of Indemnity at 4:30 a.m. on Sunday morning. He had trouble finding the town on the Internet since it was so small it did not even have a post office.

It seemed strange to him that the town's name was on the address he had been given, when they actually received their mail from the nearby town of Snyder about eight miles to the east. Kirk assumed he would find the solution to that problem when he arrived. After a little research, he found an atlas that showed the small dot on the map.

No population was written below the city limit sign. From the ten houses that occupied the town, Kirk estimated two of the houses were unoccupied so the population was probably not over fifteen.

He had seen many towns like this in Missouri that had no post office. The towns seemed pretty typical from one to the next. People seemed to move there for two reasons. The housing was affordable, and the town was quiet.

From that city limit sign Kirk estimated the distance to the other city limit sign to be 150 feet. Two roads ran through the town. The road running east and west was Highway J, which was maintained by the state and came to a dead end at the east edge of town. The other road was a sparsely graveled road that ran north off of the highway. High View Road was written on a board with letters that appeared to have been made with a can of spray paint.

"Wouldn't be much reason for anyone to stop here," commented Ron.

"I know what you mean. I'm glad we stopped at the last town and filled up."

Kirk made the left turn onto High View Road. The even numbers were on the east side of the street. There were only four houses total. One of them looked as though it had been vacant for several years. The only houses on the east side of the road were 560 and 562. Beyond that was what seemed to be a lot with nothing more than a small group of cedar trees located near the center of the property. Kirk and Ron stepped out of the car to check out the situation.

"Looks like they've moved," remarked Kirk jokingly.

"This would be the right number if there was a house there," said Ron, not sounding so sure.

"I think we may have been sent on a wild goose chase. I suppose we were foolish to believe that somewhere in this town we would be able to forget about the past." Ron almost sounded as if he would burst into tears.

"I'm going to walk for just a bit to stretch my legs."

If he's going to break down and cry, I don't want to be around. Best for him too, to be by himself and let it out.

The house adjacent to the vacant lot was a large two-story home that seemed to have been well maintained despite the fact it had been built nearly eighty years prior. Kirk walked toward the cedar trees that covered a small portion of the vacant lot. The cedars had grown up over a storm cellar. The old wooden door on the front had a lock on it but looked as though the door could have been kicked in with little effort. Kirk turned to walk back to the car and ran into a pole that was approximately six inches in diameter.

How did I miss that on my way out here?

The pole did not seem to fit in with the rest of the landscape. It was shiny, almost as though it was brand new. He noticed a small slot on the side of the pole with letters above it stating, "Insert card."

Insert card?

Kirk stood, staring blankly at the pole for several seconds.

Kirk reached into his wallet and pulled out the card the man had given him at the church. His hunch was right. As he shoved the card into the slot some sort of mechanism inside pulled the card away from him.

Just like a dollar bill changer.

Kirk heard a noise behind him as the cellar moved away, revealing a flight of highly polished, well-lit marble steps leading into the ground. He looked down the flight of stairs. The first step had "564 Indemnity" etched into the marble as if to let him know this was where he was supposed to be.

"RON. Come look at this," he shouted.

At the first shout, Ron was certain Kirk had hurt himself or had fallen into an old well.

"Ron! Ron! COME TAKE A LOOK AT THIS!"

"Holy cow . . ." were the only words Ron could speak as he looked into the cellar.

"I guess we've come this far. Might as well see who the wizard is," said Kirk as he took his first step.

Once both men were well inside the cellar, the door above them began to slide back into place. A chill ran down Kirk's spine at the thought of being trapped underground. The well-lit stairway gave Kirk little comfort for what he might find at the bottom.

CHAPTER 33

The stairway opened into a small room with a large conference table in the middle. Several small lights on the walls and a small chandelier lit the room, giving it a welcoming glow.

"Anyone home?" asked Kirk in a raised voice.

"You don't suppose they would be asleep this time of the morning, do you?" said Ron, feeling tired from the traveling and the fact he had not been up at this time of day in over a year.

A door to the side of the room suddenly opened. A large man with graying hair stepped into the room.

"Larry Kincaid," said the man holding his hand out as he walked toward them.

Wow. He looks happy. I don't think I've seen anyone ever look like he's got it so together, thought Kirk.

"Kirk Murphy . . . and this is Ron Truitt," replied Kirk, taking the liberty of introducing Ron.

"Could I interest you two gentlemen in some breakfast?" the man asked happily as though he was excited to have some company.

"I'll take you up on that offer," Ron answered quickly.

The man led them back through the door he had entered and up a slightly elevated hallway. At the end of the hallway was what appeared to be a concrete wall.

Now what's he going to do? thought Kirk.

"I have been redeemed," the man said slowly so as to allow some computerized device to recognize his voice.

Wow, looks liked the Order is up on the technology, thought Kirk.

"Have to keep our security tight," said Larry. "And always keep in mind the other side has their own organization that would like to get their hands on a few items in the Order's possession."

As the concrete wall closed behind them, Kirk realized it was the backside of a false fireplace. Once the wall was in place it looked so real Kirk would never have imagined it was a doorway.

"We're in the house next door," exclaimed Ron as he looked out the window and saw the trees that hid the cellar.

Kirk walked to the window and spotted his car.

"Better come eat while it's hot," said Larry as he started setting plates at the table.

Three plates on the table. Now how did he know how many to set out?

"What's going to happen to us now?" asked Kirk after they started to eat.

"Redemption," replied Larry with glowing eyes. "It will not be an immediate process, but it will happen in time."

"What do we have to do?" Ron said between bites of food.

"I can't tell you that. For everyone it's different. When the time comes for you to fulfill your part in the Order, you'll know what to do," Larry answered. "For me it's getting people started on their journey to forgiveness. The work of the Order is great, but no one in the Order will be given more than they can handle."

"What if we decide not to do our part?" asked Ron.

Kirk listened more intently.

"That is entirely your choice. You have free will in all aspects of your life. The fact you have come this far, for something you're not sure is possible, makes me think that when you know with all your heart you can achieve forgiveness, it's unlikely you will turn down the opportunity."

Kirk and Ron sat in thoughtful silence for the rest of the meal.

"I think I'm ready for a nap," laughed Kirk as he sat back in his chair. It had been over twenty hours since he had slept, and putting food in his stomach had made him sleepy.

"I have beds ready for both of you, but first we must start you on your journey."

Larry led them back down the stairs into the room they had first entered.

"Take a seat at the table," he instructed, pointing to the large conference table. "We will begin a ceremony that has been with the Order since the beginning. Once you drink from the cup, you will become a member of the Order."

Larry walked to the opposite side of the room and punched a code into a small keyboard-looking device on the wall. Above the keyboard were two candles mounted on the wall approximately five feet off the ground and spaced about three feet apart.

A piece of the marble wall between the two candles slid open sideways revealing an old wooden cup. Larry reached in and took the cup, holding it as though it would break if he squeezed it too tightly. Kirk saw him bow his head and heard a small whisper.

An awfully old-looking and plain cup to be put under such tight security.

Larry walked to the table and placed the cup on it. From a small pitcher sitting on the table, Larry poured water into the cup.

"Gentleman, our savior and the Order offer you freedom from the guilt you have held on to so diligently. Do you wish to drink what is offered to you?"

I came this far, thought Kirk.

"To redemption," he said as he took the cup to his mouth expecting some extreme, immediate reaction. It was like any water he had drank before.

Ron looked at him, waiting for a dramatic reaction. Kirk shrugged his shoulders as if to say, "I don't know," to the quizzical look in Ron's eyes.

Larry took the cup and filled it for Ron who drank the water without hesitation. The cup was then placed back into the wall where it had been stored.

"Gentlemen," said Larry, "I will show you to your rooms where you can get some sleep. You are now a member of the Order and are welcome in this house. You will stay here until your time to leave."

"How will we know when it's our time to leave?" asked Ron.

"You'll know."

Larry showed them to their rooms.

"I don't feel any different," Kirk confessed as Larry was leaving his room.

"You were forgiven by God when you became remorseful for your sin. If I were to take a guess I would say since you started feeling guilty you have tried hard not to do anything bad since."

"That's true," said Kirk. "I'm careful to not hurt anyone again."

Larry paused thoughtfully.

"Have you tried doing anything good for people? I finally learned to like myself when I put others' needs before my own and went out of my way to help them. When I started liking myself I realized I was a person who had done a bad thing. When I did GOOD things for people, it started outweighing the BAD thing I had done and made it seem less burdensome. The Order gave me the opportunity to do more good than I ever did harm. Redemption is given freely by God but is much harder to get from within. I see from the look in your eyes . . . you hunger for it. You will achieve it, but it won't be easy. Good luck," said Larry as he shut the door and left Kirk to his thoughts.

CHAPTER 34

Kirk walked through the back door of the church in his hometown of Lansing, Missouri.

I haven't been here for years.

The church was quiet. Prayer candles were lit at the front of the church to the left side of the altar. Kirk looked to the rear of the church at the small confessional he dreamed about as a child.

How did I get here? I'm dreaming, he suddenly realized. *I'm at the house in Indemnity, in my room, and I'm dreaming.*

"I wouldn't call this dreaming, lad. I would call it receiving a divine message."

Kirk turned quickly to see a small elderly man with short gray hair and bushy sideburns wearing a suit with a bow tie and a bowler hat.

"Do I know you?" asked Kirk, trying not to smile at the leprechaun appearance of the man, which was enhanced by the thick Irish accent.

"No, ye don't, lad. Ye can call me Joe. Always did like the name Joe. It's such a simple name. Just one syllable. People nowadays are trying to invent names that are longer and more complex than they did in the old days," he said as though he were fondly remembering a better time in his life.

"I'm Kirk, Kirk Murphy," he said, holding his hand out to shake.

"Yes, I know who ye are," acknowledged Joe, ignoring the hand. "I understand ye need redemption, and I'm here to set you on a path that will lead to that very thing. This will not be the only time I will be in touch with ye, but it will always begin in the back of this church as a reminder to ye that you are fighting yer dragon."

Kirk looked at the confessional.

"No, ye won't have any real dragons to fight this time," said Joe smiling. "Just metaphorical ones. But they can be just as big and ugly as the real ones, and they just keep getting bigger if ye don't step in and do something about them."

"How do you know so much about me?"

"I was wondering when that question would come up. It always does. I'm a messenger from God. An angel. I look like a person so yer more comfortable. I only know the things about you I need to complete the message to ye."

"So where are these metaphorical dragons I need to fight?" asked Kirk with a sick feeling growing in his stomach.

"Let's check back in the confessional. Shall we?"

Kirk opened the door to the confessional. The room was dimly light and had a slight musty odor expected of a room with only one entrance that was kept shut most of the time.

"What now?" asked Kirk.

"Take a seat, lad," replied Joe, motioning towards the empty chair reserved for the confessor.

Kirk sat down. To his immediate right was a curtain that hid the confessor from the priest for discretionary purposes. On both sides of the curtain were identical wooden chairs.

"Now if ye'll just pull the curtain back."

Kirk pulled the curtain back slowly. A face flashed before him. Underneath the curtain was a mirror with a reflection that resembled Kirk, only more hideous. Kirk fell over in terror, trying to get away from the horrible image he saw.

"WHAT THE HELL WAS THAT?" cried Kirk, his heart feeling as though it would beat out of his chest.

"That was you, lad. The bad you, anyway. The worst ye can be or have been. Before you can become a better person, ye have to understand yerself. Who ye've been, who ye are, and the potential ye have for becoming the best ye can be." Joe smiled. "We're going to start with the faults . . . weaknesses that ye know ye have and some ye don't."

I don't want to have my flaws pointed out. I know I've got plenty of them. I think I've done well ignoring them up until now . . . Huh, I never thought about that. I have ignored them. I guess I didn't want to see them.

"Ye will see these flaws from the perspective of others. Sometimes it's easier to see others' weaknesses than it is to see our own, so this should give ye a whole new perspective. Pull the curtain when yer ready, lad."

"But what . . . " Kirk looked around to see Joe was gone. "Hello . . . Joe?" Kirk shouted out into the church.

No answer.

Kirk looked back into the confessional at the curtain. The last time he was this scared, in this place, there was a thirty-foot dragon inside this tiny room. Now, himself and a mirror.

I don't want to see myself in there. I know I have flaws. They keep me up at night. Will it make a difference if I see them here?

Kirk turned towards the door. It was open as though it were calling to him, saying, "You don't have to look, just leave."

He slowly reached for the curtain with his trembling hand and ripped it down to allow full view into the mirror.

CHAPTER 35

Kirk was thrown from the small confessional room into the mirror, finding himself face to face with the most evil image of himself he had ever seen. Even the low point in his life wasn't as bad as this.

His face was horribly disfigured. Several smaller scars were visible on his lower cheek but failed to compare to the large one that ran across his right eye. It began just below the bottom of his hairline near the center of his forehead and down the right side of his face to less than an inch away from the corner of his mouth.

"So, you decided to take a hard look at yourself?" asked his evil-looking twin. "You sure you want to see your flaws?" His glowing eyes and satisfied smile pushed the scar upward on his face.

"How come when I look at you I don't see myself?" asked Kirk, avoiding his question.

"You see yourself," replied his twin. "But it's the part of yourself you've been able to look past, avoid, pretend as though I don't exist. But you know me, Kirk. I do exist."

Kirk looked at the ground. *He's not me. That is not me.*

"Every time you've ever hated, the flaws in your character you've been unable to control, that's me, or should I say YOU. As much as you struggled to look past me, you're going to be unable to avoid it now. LOOK AT ME!"

The sudden harshness in his tone caused Kirk to look up to find himself no longer facing his twin but instead facing a young Kirk Murphy who was standing on the playground with his best friend, Jeff Lorrell.

I wish they would leave me alone. Kirk could hear the thought and feel emotions that were not his.

Don't cry in front of them. Kirk could hear the thoughts, but he had no control over them.

"Why don't you stop being such a doofus?" said Kirk's younger self.

"And take a bath, dummy," added Jeff.

"Good one, man," said Kirk, giving Jeff a high five.

"Let's leave the nerd alone and go play."

The young Kirk and Jeff ran off, leaving him to the thoughts that were flashing through his mind.

"Jim Lather," Kirk thought. "I'm Jim Lather."

Kirk had almost forgotten how they used to torment the poor kid. He came from a bad home. Kirk remembered his parents talking about the police showing up at his house when they thought he wasn't listening. Kirk walked over to the side of the school and began crying. Emotions and thoughts that belonged to Jim overwhelmed him.

"Why do they pick on me?" Suddenly a wave of emotion avalanched him. Scenes of his parents abusing him, other children picking on him for the way he acted, even teachers misunderstanding this poor child whose life was totally out of his own control.

His mind is a horrible place to be. And I made it worse. I picked on him because I thought it looked cool to the other kids. I knew it was wrong, and I did it anyway when I could have made his life better with a nice word or friendship.

"Starting to remember who I am?"

Kirk looked up to see his evil twin smiling.

"We done a number on that kid. Did you see how miserable he was? You might have forced it out of your mind that it ever happened, but I'll bet he didn't."

A sick feeling ran through Kirk's body.

Why wasn't I strong enough to be a friend to him when he needed one so badly?

"You think you hate yourself for that?" said his twin. "Get a load of this next flaw."

CHAPTER 36

"Are you taking your parents' car out this weekend?"

Kirk was looking at a teenage version of himself. A group of kids standing nearby seemed slightly amused at the comment.

I don't want to hear what I'm about to say.

Cynthia Preston. I'm Cynthia Preston, thought Kirk.

I wish this dumb ass would just leave me the hell alone. I know I wrecked my parents' car. Just leave me alone. Kirk winced at the thoughts directed toward him.

Worst of all he could feel Cynthia's embarrassment. She wanted to tell him to shut up and go away, but with the large group being amused at her expense she walked away, degraded. Cynthia turned and left the younger Kirk standing there "full of himself" in front of the group of teenagers he had amused at Cynthia's expense. A feeling of shame overtook him as the memory of her parents finding out about the wreck came to him.

She came home that evening knowing they would overreact to the news.

"We trusted you with the car and look how that turned out. No driving for you except to school and back."

Her self-esteem was already as low as it had been in her young life, but he managed to drop it more without even realizing what he had done until this moment eight years later.

I was so cruel without even thinking about it. Trying to make everyone laugh and not giving any thought to the one person who didn't laugh. HOW? How could I have been so annoying, so cruel, and not realize the power I had? The power to give encouragement and raise feelings of self-worth and the power to take it away with nothing but words. I'm so embarrassed. I hope I don't have to see every time I made someone feel that way. I know there are plenty of others. It was all words. Somehow I managed to pick the wrong ones.

"How do ya like me now?"

Kirk looked up to see his twin.

"You disgust me. I hate everything about you. I HATE YOU!" Kirk lunged toward his twin, grabbing him by the throat and pushing him to the ground. Kirk gripped his hands tightly around his twin's throat. "I HATE YOU! Everything about you makes me sick to my stomach."

Despite the pressure Kirk was exerting on his throat, his twin was smiling, pleased at the angry reaction he was getting from Kirk.

"You can't get rid of me. We're not even close to done yet."

CHAPTER 37

He sure is in a hurry to get done. I wish I could keep up with his pace. Kirk heard the thoughts as he saw himself filling in a posthole for a fence he was building. The younger Kirk looked to be sixteen years old. But the thoughts belonged to the older man beside him. *I'm Grandpa!*

Kirk had good memories of working beside his grandpa on the farm. He died after Kirk left for Washington. Standing here in his grandfather's shoes, he sensed his grandpa felt the same about working beside him.

"If you slow down, you'll do a better job and be able to last all day."

"If I slow down, we won't get done." Kirk never even looked at his grandpa as he continued shoveling dirt into the hole.

I sure wish he would listen to some of my advice. I used to act like that towards my grandpa when he tried to tell me something. Sure miss working with him. Hope Kirk enjoys this the way I used to enjoy working with grandpa. Would have saved me a world of trouble if I had learned things from him instead of on my own. Seventy-one years of knowledge and this sixteen year old boy thinks he has things figured out better than me, Kirk heard his grandpa think.

It never occurred to me that Grandpa might be thinking back to a similar time in his life. I can tell from the way Grandpa feels he enjoyed working with me.

I remember when I thought I had all of it figured out, he heard his grandpa thinking. *I think if I lived two hundred more years I still wouldn't scratch the surface on figuring things out. But I do need to try to pass on to this kid something he can use and maybe it will save him some grief.*

Kirk was surprised at how urgent his grandpa felt about talking to him. A memory of his mom asking his grandpa to talk to him about his excessive drinking flashed before him.

"Kirk, I need you to stop working for a minute so we can talk."

"Go ahead," replied Kirk, still trying to finish packing the dirt in.

"Kirk, I need you to stop working and talk."

Kirk stopped for a minute. "What's up?"

"I hear tell that you enjoy drinking a lot. Is that true?"

"Who said that?" responded Kirk, trying to dodge the first question with a question of his own.

"That's not important," argued his grandpa, understanding that Kirk avoiding the question was as good as a yes.

"You know, Kirk," his grandpa went on, "I've seen a lot of good men in my time who let the drinking get the best of them. It turned good men into something they were not meant to be. It's one thing to have a drink after a hard day's work. It's another to live for it. Don't let drinking ruin your life, Kirk. Do you understand what I'm saying?"

"I don't have a drinking problem, Grandpa. I'm okay. I have to go get ready to meet the guys in town. I'll come back out Monday and help work on the fence some more." Kirk almost ran to his truck.

I avoided that whole conversation.

"Sorry, Betty. I don't think he heard a word I said," remarked Kirk's grandpa to his mom as though she were standing right there.

He's right. I didn't even remember the conversation until now. I handled every situation I didn't want to deal with exactly like that, thought Kirk as he saw himself running off to his truck.

Get out when it gets tough. Man, what a disappointment I am. Grandpa tried to stop me. I just wouldn't listen. Sorry, Grandpa. At least you tried. You sure had your work cut out for you, though.

Kirk's grandpa picked up the shovel with a heavy heart and finished the work he had left behind.

CHAPTER 38

Let's head home now. We're going to be pushing it if we drive to the other side of town and have to head back after we stop for a while."

Kirk quickly glanced up to see himself, drunk and unwilling to listen to reason.

I'm Sarah.

"Come on. We're only young once. Let's enjoy it," he heard himself say.

OH, NO. This is the night Sarah died. The night of the wreck. I don't want to . . . I . . . I can't go through this again.

"Come on, Kirk. Let's go home," pleaded Sarah.

There's no way he's going to listen to you, Sarah, thought Kirk as he recognized the same look he had given his grandpa when he didn't listen to him.

There's no way he's going to listen to me, thought Sarah almost simultaneously.

Sorry, Sarah. I see how I am now, if it helps any.

Kirk saw himself stumble as he turned and walked to the truck. A sick, uneasy feeling ran through Sarah as she debated on taking a stand and threatening to stay here if Kirk didn't let her drive. She gave in, realizing when Kirk was drunk like he was now he wouldn't listen.

STOP HIM, SARAH! Kirk tried to scream the thought, hoping it would be loud enough for Sarah to hear.

MAKE THAT IDIOT STOP!

He won't listen to me. For an instant Kirk thought she might have heard him.

I know you were probably thinking the same thing, Sarah. Just like before when we knew I wouldn't listen. I love you, and I'm sorry.

Kirk was almost certain she couldn't hear him but decided it would be best, at least for his own sanity, to stop trying to talk to her.

How could I not listen to her? All she wanted was to go home. She would still be alive if I had listened.

The ride to the party was quiet as Kirk listened to Sarah's last thoughts. He was sitting in the middle of the truck as Sarah always had, next to himself. He could see Sarah's reflection in the mirror.

I always wished I would have another chance to see her. Just to look into her eyes again. Now I wish I didn't get the chance. Not like this. Not on this night.

The party was torture for him and Sarah. He could hear her thoughts and feel her anxiousness.

Only forty-five minutes until her curfew. Only about thirty until she dies. I thought I was having such a good time. She was miserable. All she wanted was to go home early enough that I wasn't hammered so she could get a decent good night kiss and a nice word about how I felt about her. Why was I so selfish?

To add to his misery, he saw himself, the drunken fool. He never had this opportunity to see himself when he was drinking.

I love him, but he is so stupid when he's drunk, he heard Sarah thinking.

The words cut him. Not because they were harsh, but because they were true.

Look at me. I thought I was having such a good time. What an idiot.

Now through Sarah's eyes, in her final hours, he saw the fool he had been when he was drinking. Hell, he saw it in the way the other people at the party were reacting to him. Rolling their eyes at his comments, the whispers between people who were far enough from him not to be heard.

Kirk saw himself walk towards a tall skinny kid that had a group of six people standing around him listening intently to his story about taking a three-week bull-riding course over the summer.

"Hey, Bill, I'm on my third night of drinking . . . went out with . . . "

"Hold on a second, Kirk. I need to get in my truck and get a cold one. I'll get back with ya," Bill said as he turned away, not giving Kirk time to respond.

Wow . . . he didn't want to talk to me at all. I'm all but sure he didn't try to come back to see what I had to say, either. Guess I could have taken the time to listen to his story instead of trying to top it with one of my own. His was better. When I think back on it, many people avoided conversation with me. Guess they preferred someone who's not an idiot to talk to. I see I ran the rest of the group off also.

Two of the guys from the group had walked over near Sarah.

"Wow, that guy don't shut up. Kind of hard to get a word in."

Sarah turned and walked away.

Oh, my God. She's embarrassed. I can feel it. Half an hour until she dies and I'm being such a dumb ass that she's embarrassed to be seen with me. Why didn't I see this? Why do I have to be someone else to see my faults, my shortcomings. I don't want her to die seeing me this way.

"It's all right, lad."

Kirk looked up to see his true reflection in the confessional mirror. Joe, and not his evil twin, was standing next to him.

"I THOUGHT THIS WAS SUPPOSED TO HELP! TO HELL WITH THIS, JOE! This sucks," Kirk exclaimed in a voice indicating his anger was turning to frustration, despair, and the depths of misery. "Am I that horrible? I knew I had flaws, but am I that . . . ?" Kirk couldn't finish the sentence through the lump in his throat as he thought about the horrible person he witnessed in the mirror.

"It's harsh to see, lad, but that's who ye are. It's yer humanity," replied Joe simply.

"Is that what it means to be human?" shouted Kirk with an angry tone. "To spend the first part of your life acting like an idiot so you can look in a mirror years later and realize how stupid you were? I knew I wasn't an intelligent man, but that mirror helped me realize what potential was true."

"Bad and good, lad," remarked Joe. "That's what your humanity gives you. We had to show you the flaws you have. No matter how horrible they are to look at ye must recognize them to become the person God wishes for you to be, to reach yer potential so Kirk Murphy will never be that person again. Now, lad, I want to show ye the good side of Kirk Murphy. The traits ye have that are positive."

"I can't . . . not right now, anyway. I need some time to think about what I've seen."

Without an answer from Joe, Kirk woke up in his bed. He sat up suddenly, confused.

Right, he thought, *I'm still in Indemnity.*

Kirk pulled the covers up over himself and pulled his pillow close to his chest.

CHAPTER 39

Ron Truitt looked down at his hands confused about the child crying in his arms.

Where is Ron? He should have been home hours ago, Ron heard the thought. *I'm Nancy.*

Oh, no. Not on this night, Ron thought as the realization hit him this was the night she left him.

Ron noticed his two-year-old sitting in the middle of the floor playing with the trash that littered the floor.

How did we live like this? I'm so sorry, kids . . . Nancy, I . . . I didn't realize it was this bad.

The more the baby cried, the more he could feel Nancy's anxiety growing.

I can't do this anymore, Ron. I can't take it. Neither can they.

Ron sensed she had been entertaining the thought of leaving for some time. Suddenly the door opened.

Oh, my God. He looks trashed.

Even Ron was surprised at how terrible he looked. He had never taken a good look at how bad he had become at this, his lowest point. It was obvious from the way he looked he rarely used a mirror at this point in his life.

I didn't realize I had sunk that low. He felt a sense of fear growing in Nancy. *She's terrified of me.*

Ron felt a deep sense of shame as the emotion struck him. She almost let him go back to the bedroom without asking about the milk and diapers because she was so afraid of his possible reaction.

"Ron, where are the diapers and milk?" He heard her force the words out.

He couldn't believe the look on his face. It was obvious it was the furthest thing from his mind.

I can't believe the drugs were more important than the kids.

"Oh, Ron. Did you buy more drugs? How are we going to buy food and pay the rent? We have to stop living like this."

"Are you blaming me for this? You could do something once in a while, too. Why don't you get the damn milk?"

Please don't make me watch the rest of this, pleaded Ron, hoping someone was listening.

He had played this whole scene over in his mind a hundred times, but this was the first time he was able to see it from Nancy's perspective.

"It has to stop, Ron. We can't live like this. The kids can't live like this."

Nancy was forcing herself to be strong. He could feel how badly she wanted to get through to him. To change him so these children would have a dad. Not one that wanted to be left alone to his drugs, but one that would tuck them in at night after reading them a story. One who would take them out in the yard and throw the ball around. She was trying to give him his last chance to be a good dad.

"GET OUT OF MY WAY!" He saw himself push her as if to say he didn't want or deserve that chance.

The baby! Ron heard Nancy's mind scream as she dropped the baby on her way to the floor.

"We sure screwed that up, didn't we?"

Ron looked up to see an evil image of himself smiling in the mirror.

CHAPTER 40

"Morning, Kirk," said Larry with a smile. "Or should I say good afternoon."

"What time is it?"

"Five thirty. You slept right through lunch. I thought you needed your sleep more than you needed food."

"Good call, Larry. I was beat."

"I've got some people downstairs I would like for you to meet. You may want to change into your regular clothes."

"Oh, sure," responded Kirk, suddenly realizing he was in an old pair of sweats and a T-shirt he used as pajamas. "I'll be right back."

Kirk hurried up the stairs and changed into more presentable clothing.

"I'm ready," announced Kirk as he burst back into the kitchen.

"That was fast."

"Always have been fast at getting ready, Larry. I think I should attribute most of that to the fact I rarely give much thought to how I look."

Larry seemed amused by the comment.

As they walked down the steps, Kirk could hear people talking below. The voices sounded almost festive.

"Attention everyone," announced Larry, trying to calm the group of five who were sitting around the table. "I would like for you to meet one of the newest members of the Order, Kirk Murphy. Kirk, I will let everyone introduce themselves because I can't remember all of their names."

Everyone sitting at the table gave Kirk a warm smile.

"Hello, Kirk. Garrett Lavor," declared a middle-aged man sitting at the head of the table.

I think I caught a little bit of an accent. Maybe Minnesota, thought Kirk.

"From the look on your face I can tell Larry failed to explain why we're here. Now try to forgive him, he does a good job but he's incredibly underpaid."

This comment seemed to amuse the others sitting at the table.

"You're not sure why we're here, let me explain. The initiation you recently underwent is performed at this location once a year on the same date. Every five years we are invited back to celebrate our redemption and help you on the path to yours. Kind of a support group. We sit around and compare guilt. Let each other know we're not alone. Not to make anyone stand out, just so we recognize our humanity. We recognize that none of us have the right to judge the others. We all sinned. We all are forgiven."

Garrett cocked his head back and scratched his chin nervously. His large eyes darted across both sides of the table as though he were making sure everyone was paying attention and there might be trouble if someone wasn't.

"I sold drugs, Kirk. This may not sound so bad to some of you, but listen up. I had a good business going. Kind of a regional man with lots of people under me, a wholesaler. One day I got this call from my sister. Seems her teenage daughter overdosed on crack. I swore to my sister I would find out who sold it to her and make 'em pay. To make a long story short, it was me. They lived outta state, but one of my people branched out into their state. I sold it to him. He sold it to my niece. I killed her. Got me to thinking about the other people I sold to. How many died I didn't even think about?"

Garrett's words seemed as though they came from a man who would be tortured with guilt, but his face showed a different story . . . one that said, "I screwed up, but I can't torture myself forever."

"This is my tenth anniversary of my redemption and I hope to see you in five years," he said, pointing his finger at Kirk. "You'll make it, pal."

"Linda Manchester. This is my fifth anniversary," said the woman to Garrett's left.

Kirk estimated her to be about thirty years old. She was an attractive woman with dark hair. Her eyes had the same look of cleanness he had seen in Larry's. Linda pushed herself away from the table to reveal she was sitting in a wheelchair. A blanket covered her legs.

"Nice to meet you," said Linda, holding her hand out. She gave Kirk a look that said, "I know."

"Nice to meet you," said Kirk not knowing what look he was supposed to give back.

"I used to enjoy drinking. A lot," said Linda. "What would it hurt? I asked myself. I never drank at work. Sure, I might come in with a hangover, but I was usually over it by ten in the morning. Sometimes the girls I worked with would go out after work and have a few drinks. Pretty harmless. My husband, Brad, worked second shift. I came home after a few drinks with the girls. Brad went to work, leaving me with our eighteen-month-old boy, Jeromy. Wouldn't you know it? We were out of liquor at home. What did I do? What else could I do? I packed up Jeromy and headed to the liquor store. We never made it. We crashed into a power pole. I put Jeromy into his car seat but apparently I was too wasted to make sure the belt clicked. He didn't make it, and neither did my legs or my marriage. My husband was always aggravated by my drinking and tried to talk me into quitting, but the death of our son was more than our marriage could stand."

That explains the look she gave me, thought Kirk, realizing the similarity of their situations.

Linda looked to her left at the woman sitting next to her as if to say, "Your turn."

"Pat Layne," said the elderly lady impatiently, as though she had somewhere to be. "This is my thirty-fifth anniversary." The expression on her face changed from impatient to a look of pride at the amount of time she had been in the Order. "Kirk, it's nice to meet you," she said, giving Kirk a warm smile. "This is my seventh meeting, eight including my initiation. I suppose by now you realize you're not alone. We've all strayed at one time or another. For whatever reason you're here, it's time to move on, Kirk."

I wonder what this sweet old lady did. I would have expected her to be home baking cookies for the grandkids. Guess she must have endured a lot of guilt to have earned a place in this organization. Everyone else so far has.

Pat looked at the gentleman sitting next to her. "I'm done," she said plainly.

Guess I'm not going to find out what she did. Doesn't seem like whatever she did almost forty years ago matters much in her life at the present. Gives me a little hope I'll get past this. Might hit her up later about how long it was before she stopped feeling guilty.

"Jim Richardson," said the short man to Pat's left. "Had an uncle who had quite a collection of pornographic material. He allowed me to view almost anything at anytime. I was young when I first started hanging out with him. Mom thought it was okay because he was my dad's brother. Looking back, I suppose he had a problem also. You wouldn't believe how bad porn will screw up your mind. It's as much of an addiction as any drug you can think of. All I thought about all the time was sex and how I could either get it or find a place that sold porn so I could at least watch it. When it was all said and done, I estimate I wasted fifteen years on it. And I mean wasted," he said, emphasizing the way he felt about his previous life. "Hours I spent in front of the television and porn shops feeding my mind the material it craved. Money and time down the drain." Jim paused. "Funny, the more I searched for material, the more I craved a variety of sexual material. It's not too far from porn that most of us would consider 'normal' to child pornography. Just got to get in with the wrong people. Once the thought comes into your mind the fantasies start. I think it's the same with any sin or addiction. It starts so small you don't even notice it's there. Then without any conscious consent it's grown into something horrible. I used to be a child molester." Jim almost blurted it out as though he meant to ease into it a little easier, but there was no way to let it out without shocking everyone.

A sick feeling came to Kirk at the thought of this man molesting children.

No way! He doesn't deserve to be forgiven. The thought came to Kirk instinctively. He had never stood before someone he knew had committed such a horrendous deed. Such a lack of morality. He heard Jim's story, start to finish, and the fact he started at a young age viewing porn. Kirk knew there were a lot of psychological factors involved in his circumstances. Jim probably couldn't understand, but when Kirk heard the words in his own mind, "He doesn't deserve to be forgiven," he understood how people must feel about him.

Perspective, he thought. *How many people said those words about me?*

His life came to a point that was out of control. *One missed step,* he thought to himself. *When did I have the choice to stop it?*

"I'm clean now, but it took so long to become that way. I suppose it's the nature of addictions. It takes a long time to be able to overcome the addiction and even longer before your mind stops screaming for it. I've been clean for ten years now, and I make sure to steer clear of anything that might lead me back to my addiction," said Jim. "There is hope for you, Kirk. Do what the Order asks of you to the best of your ability. There is redemption for you." Jim smiled as he thought back to some point when he first felt redeemed. Pat reached over and gently squeezed Jim's hand.

Kirk felt at home among these five strangers. He had given up long ago on finding anyone to talk to that understood him, and now he was in a room filled with people who had been through situations as bad or possibly worse than his own.

"Very well," said Larry after an uncomfortable pause. "I'm glad to see all of you made it back for your anniversaries. Feel free to roam around the town." Larry turned and walked up the stairs leaving the five of them alone.

"Why don't we take that walk around town, Kirk?" asked Linda.

"I've seen the whole town," Kirk replied. "There really isn't that much to see."

"I know," said Linda, sounding a little aggravated. "But the weather's nice and we should be enjoying it. Now, grab my wheelchair and push me out."

"How can I say no to that?" said Kirk, trying to lighten the mood.

Linda smiled at the comment.

"You would think the Order would be ADA compliant," Linda said trying to match Kirk's humor as he pulled her up the steps. "It's a good thing to help someone anytime you can," Linda said in a more serious tone. "It's also good to know when it's time to let someone help you."

I don't think I would make it, thought Kirk. *I've never been good at asking for help, even when I knew I needed it.*

"So where are you from?" inquired Linda, trying to pull some conversation out of him.

"A small town in Missouri. I live in Washington now," replied Kirk, realizing he had not been much on conversation. "How about you?"

"Lake View, North Dakota. Sort of a small town. I never lived anywhere else. I guess I was born with roots. Scared me to even leave long enough to come here to Indemnity the first time."

Kirk opened the front door of the house. The town was filled with people. Music was coming from a stage set up on the south end of High View Road and all the way down the street to the north lights that were blinking where vendors sold refreshments and carnival-type games were being played.

Where the hell did all these people come from? There must be five hundred or more.

"You didn't think only four of us were having our anniversary, did you?"

"I didn't consider everyone with an anniversary would show up."

"The four of us were asked by Mr. Kincaid to meet with you. I suppose each one for a different reason. I was probably chosen because of our similar situations."

"I was thinking that might be the case."

"This is a celebration for those of us who have been redeemed, Kirk. We made it through our trials, and now we celebrate our freedom from guilt. I know it's tough for you to feel like celebrating now, but in five years when you come back here—and you will come back—you will see this celebration in a different way than you see it now. It will be better, Kirk. By the time you're done with all you need to do, you will know who you are. You will understand what things you need to do to make yourself happy."

Kirk walked by a man who tried to encourage him to throw three darts and win a prize. Kirk smiled. "No, thanks."

"Before I was introduced to the Order," Linda continued, "I was focused on alcohol. I thought I needed it, after a hard day at work, the kid was too fussy, it was my day off, or whatever the excuse of the day was. You know when I was a kid I used to have goals and dreams. I was a good runner. I had a good chance at running in the Olympics. I had some talent, but I worked hard for every medal I earned. It made me feel," Linda paused, trying to use the right word, "it made me feel alive. That was it . . . alive. The dreams came to a halt for me. I fell in love and married young. We had a child when I was twenty. I guess that was when I thought I was supposed to stop my life to raise the kid and be a wife. We had a decent marriage, or at least I thought everything was okay. When our marriage was almost over, my husband told me that was one of the things he used to love about me—the way I dreamed about something and then did it. I didn't realize I could still have my own goals and be a good wife and mother. Somewhere along the way my dreams were gone and alcohol took its place. Do you have any dreams, Kirk?"

"Not really. I haven't had much of a desire since the accident."

"You need dreams, Kirk. Achievable dreams with goals that are hard—not impossible, but hard. That's what life is about. God doesn't want us moping around feeling sorry for ourselves when we screw up. He wants us to push ourselves, use all the gifts and talent he's given us and put it into some project we enjoy. That's our way of glorifying him. We need to push ourselves to our limits and remember that our accomplishments are for his glory. I used to let the past weigh me down. Now life is so good. I've never felt this satisfied."

Wow. She's got it figured out. I hope I can make it to that point someday. What she's saying makes a lot of sense.

Kirk looked up and found he had pushed Linda to the edge of town, past the lights and the noise. He was enjoying listening to her so much he barely noticed where they were.

"Guess we better turn and go back," suggested Kirk.

"Let's stay here for a little while . . . it's so peaceful. I just want to look at the stars." She looked up at Kirk, her blue eyes looking quizzically at him as she brushed her long black hair out of her face.

I think she wants to spend a little time with just me away from the crowd.

"That sounds wonderful," Kirk said, looking at her with a smile.

Linda turned her head upward with a gleam in her eyes, trying to bite her top lip to hold back the expression she was afraid would give away how happy she was that he wanted to stay out here also.

"It is peaceful out here," said Kirk, realizing he had not been this much into a conversation in years. Linda was so full of life, and she was the type of person that made you feel like she had answers. She didn't pretend to have all of them, but the ones she did have she seemed sure of.

Kirk pushed her next to a large flat rock at the side of the road.

"Think of a goal you would like to achieve, Kirk."

Kirk thought hard. "I don't know."

"Come on. You've thought of something in the past that might be fun to try."

Kirk laughed at the thought that came to his mind.

"What? What did you think of?" asked Linda, realizing he had thought of something he wanted to do by the look on his face.

"Oh, nothing. It's silly."

"It's not silly. Tell me."

Kirk hesitated. "You won't laugh, will you?"

"No. I promise," she replied, hoping that whatever he said didn't cause her to laugh uncontrollably.

"I've never even flown in one, but I think I would like to get my license to fly a hot air balloon. It seems like it would be such a good way to get away from all the things that weigh me down. Like if I was up there I would be too high for any problem I have down here to reach me.

Does that seem silly?" he asked, looking for confirmation that the only goal he could think of wasn't stupid.

"That sounds perfect," she said with a look of amazement.

CHAPTER 41

Kirk pushed Linda back toward the lights of the festival. They had spent several hours talking at the edge of town.

"Hey, Kirk, quite a party, wouldn't you say?"

Kirk turned to see Ron holding one of the largest stuffed rabbits he had ever seen and a stick of cotton candy.

"Hey, Ron, how about this?"

"Something to look forward to in five years. I know you were wondering if you would get to see me again, now it looks like you may be fortunate enough to see me every five years. How about that?" said Ron, smiling.

"Puts my mind at ease, Ron," said Kirk playing along.

"I better get to the games. I hear they're closing this place down in a half hour or so." Ron walked away at a brisk pace, causing the bunny's ears to flop up and down in a way that amused Kirk.

"It's so hard to watch them grow up," joked Kirk.

Linda laughed. "You've got a good sense of humor."

Kirk had not joked much with anyone for a long time. In fact, after seeing the failed humor of the "Cynthia Preston" episode in the mirror, he had sworn off humor completely. But with Linda, he let his guard down. The last person he had felt this at ease around was Sarah.

"Are they going to close down soon?" asked Kirk.

"We have to be out by three in the morning, and it's almost two," replied Linda with a tone that said, "I don't want it to end either."

"Better push me to my car, Kirk. I think it's time for me to go." The thought of leaving was making her feel worse than actually leaving would so she decided it was time to go.

Kirk pushed her to a large van equipped to accommodate Linda's wheelchair. He was impressed as he watched her load herself into the van, climb into the driver's seat, and start the vehicle.

"It was nice talking with you," she said, looking out the window.

"You, too, Linda," replied Kirk with a forced smile. He felt sad to see her go.

"Look me up if you're ever near Lake View."

"You can bet on it," said Kirk, leaning against the door.

Linda's face softened. "Goodbye, Kirk," she whispered, leaning towards him.

Kirk's heart skipped a beat. He wanted to say goodbye, but almost instinctively moved closer. Linda stopped inches from Kirk as if to say, "You sure you want to do that?" Kirk replied by moving the rest of the way. Their lips met briefly, with a passion Kirk had not felt for a long time.

Linda pulled away first. "See ya, Kirk," said Linda as she put the van in drive.

"Bye" was the only word Kirk could force out as he watched her drive away.

CHAPTER 42

Kirk looked at himself in the mirror. He was alone in the confessional. His evil image was still fresh in his mind, but the image in front of him was his true reflection.

"What's good about me?" Kirk said.

"Well, that's real nice. If someone had asked me the bad things about me, I could have thought of something. Always looking for the bad. There I go . . . I see one of my faults is I look for the bad in things more than the good."

"That could be a good quality depending on the circumstance," commented Joe, walking into the tiny room.

"What do you mean?"

"Ye look for the bad in yerself sometimes harder than ye should, but when ye find it ye always try to correct it to better yerself. Striving to improve yerself is a good quality."

"I didn't think about it that way," acknowledged Kirk, nodding approvingly at Joe's version of what he had considered to be a fault.

"Now what?" asked Kirk.

"Time to see the good side of Kirk Murphy."

Kirk turned to the mirror again. His reflection appeared to be a younger version of himself. *I look about sixteen,* he thought. It had been a long time since he had seen his reflection without his brow being wrinkled as though he were deep in thought or without some of the lines that were starting to show.

"Hello, Kirk," said his twin in a pleasant voice.

Kirk found himself in the room alone with his good twin the way he had with his evil twin. He was both amused and intrigued at the younger-looking version of himself. It was strange to see himself that way—without the guilt, before life started wearing him down.

"You can be this way on the inside," stated his twin. "You will see me when you look in the mirror, but you will have to work for it and you will have to understand who I am."

The world around Kirk changed. He found himself on the school bus watching a fifteen-year-old version of himself getting on the bus looking for a seat.

"Hey, Derrick," said Kirk's younger version to an athletic fellow who was one of the popular kids in school.

"Hey, Kirk," replied Derrick. "Did you have a good weekend?" Derrick winked.

Kirk smiled at the comment, remembering he and Derrick had hung out on Saturday night.

He won't sit by me or even pretend to know me.

Kirk heard the thought. He felt a nervous feeling as though this person he was inside of was unaccustomed to positive feedback from others. Kirk saw his younger version look directly at him and smile. The nervous feeling left as he sat down in the same seat.

"How about you, Traci, did you have a good weekend?" his younger version said with a warm smile.

Traci Paterson, thought Kirk. *I'm Traci Paterson.*

Traci was considered to be in with the not-so-popular people in school. Most people barely knew she existed. It was so much easier for them to walk by her than to say anything to her.

Kirk felt a smile cross Traci's face and a feeling that this kind of attention was rare and welcomed.

"Not too bad," said Traci.

Kirk could see her memory of sitting around the house with her parents playing board games on Saturday night.

"You didn't overdo it with the booze, did you?" said his younger version jokingly, knowing Traci probably never touched alcohol.

Traci smiled shyly.

Kirk couldn't believe how starved Traci was for this kind of attention. He had trouble comprehending he had made her feel so good just by talking with her on the way to school.

"You didn't even realize how important just having a conversation with her was, did you?" asked Kirk's twin.

Kirk could barely answer, still in awe at the way he had made Traci feel.

"I . . . I didn't realize . . ."

"That was you at fifteen, Kirk. You hung out with the kids who were considered more popular on one night, but on the next day you weren't afraid of what they would think if you hung out with those people they considered to be less popular. You didn't care what they thought. You didn't see people as categories like less popular or more popular. Rich or poor. They were never your tags for people. You saw everyone as human. Athletes, nerds, and outcasts. Society's words. You knew, Kirk. Deep down, you knew they were all the same. For some reason, you got it when a lot of other people didn't. You understood they all mattered."

A smile crossed Kirk's face. He could feel his eyes glowing at the realization he viewed people that way. No one more important than the other.

"I can tell by the look on your face you enjoyed that," said his twin. "There's more."

CHAPTER 43

"Oh, no! Come on . . . start." Kirk found himself turning the ignition of an early model Chevy that was beginning to slow as though the battery was running down. Kirk could hear himself saying the words, but he did not release them.

"Look at the fuel gauge. It's empty," said a woman in the front seat who sounded somewhat distressed.

Kirk could tell from the uncertainty he felt that whoever he was felt distressed also.

I don't think I've seen these people before, thought Kirk.

"What are we going to do, Ben? It's five miles to the nearest town, and it doesn't look like too many people come down this road at this time of night. Ben, the baby woke up."

"I heard."

The infant in the woman's arms began crying loudly as though the child sensed the desperation his parents were feeling. Kirk felt a tinge of uncertainty as the man saw headlights coming over the hill.

"Someone's coming, Jill."

As the man looked into the car, Kirk could see the woman look back as the lights came across her face. She held her baby closer to her.

That's my old truck, thought Kirk to himself as the vehicle pulled to a stop beside him. *Been a while since the old truck looked so good. Almost looks brand new.*

I remember stopping to help these people, thought Kirk as the memory came to him. *I was on my way home from Sarah's house.*

"Need some help?" asked Kirk's younger version with a friendly smile that seemed to ease the feeling and looks of concern.

"We ran out of gas. I thought I could make it to Eastville to fill up. Guess I should have filled up sooner. But we were in such a hurry to make it home. Been visiting the wife's family down in Arkansas. Being in a hurry sure cost us a lot of time," Ben said, feeling less isolated now that Kirk had showed up.

"I live a couple miles up the road," remarked Kirk. "I can run home and fill up our gas can from our fuel barrel, which should give you more than enough fuel to get to Eastville."

Ben breathed a sigh of relief as a solution had come to their dire situation—the feeling his family was going to be all right overwhelmed him.

"He's going to get us some fuel, Jill," Ben said reassuringly. "We'll be on our way home soon."

Jill smiled at her husband as the look of concern left her face. She kissed her child's forehead. "Thank you," she whispered, looking at the taillights of Kirk's truck.

"You never thought twice about stopping to help them, did you?"

Kirk found himself facing his twin.

"I knew they were grateful, but I never realized the emotion they were feeling at the time."

Kirk glanced up to find himself talking to his true reflection. A smile crossed his face.

"Maybe you're not so bad, ol boy."

Kirk saw one reflection. One that was a mixture of the good and bad he had witnessed.

"Me," he said to himself. "They were both me."

CHAPTER 44

Ron found himself sitting in a rocking chair holding a baby. He could tell the baby was his oldest child.

This was quite a few years back, Ron thought to himself.

"Hey, Nancy, can I have a turn?"

It was a younger, shaven, and cleaner version of himself. Ron could tell from Nancy's feelings she was ready to go back to bed and was grateful for the help.

He's a good dad, she thought as she paused for a few minutes to enjoy the view of the man she was still deeply in love with.

I remember when I was like this, Ron thought to himself.

The memory of how good it felt to hold their infant baby and rock him to sleep came back to him. He enjoyed hearing Nancy's thoughts of how good of a dad she thought he was. He had almost forgotten how good it used to feel to be this way.

"That was nice. Wasn't it?" said his twin.

Ron looked at him with a new determination in his eyes.

"I was a good dad. I can be that dad. If I ever get the chance again, I won't blow it."

CHAPTER 45

Kirk walked between the wooden pews reflecting the dim lighting making its way through the stained glass windows. His footsteps, though muffled by the thin carpet, seemed to echo loudly in the otherwise quiet church. The door to the small room near the back of the church slowly opened as he approached it.

"Hello, lad. Did you enjoy your look in the mirror?" asked Joe.

Kirk couldn't help but smile at the short man with the long sideburns and matching Irish accent.

"Now I'm going to show you a man who's about to reach a breaking point in his life like the one you reached the night Sarah died," declared Joe, not waiting for his answer. "Let's step out the door for a minute."

Kirk followed Joe through the door of the church, which to Kirk's surprise led them to the inside of a bar. He looked around, confused. People were drinking, and a band was playing on a small stage, across the smoke-filled room.

Kirk turned to look back in the church to end this scenario his mind was having trouble comprehending. He did not need to open the door. The wooden door that seconds before was now glass no longer led back inside the church but into a dimly lit street with a steady flow of traffic.

"Ye might never get used to that," said Joe, smiling as though he enjoyed the confusion this situation caused him. "Ye'll do well to remember you're still in a house in South Dakota."

"That's right. I forgot this is a dream."

"Not a dream, lad. This is your instructions for a mission that if accepted will directly affect the outcome of your life and other people's lives. So ye need to listen close. Everything I say, and everything ye see, is important. We are at a bar in Elam, Texas, called Steve's Place. It's Friday. Four days from today."

"You're telling me what I'm seeing isn't going to take place for four more days?" asked Kirk, trying to comprehend the fact he was seeing the future.

"Yes. You've probably heard it referred to as prophesy, if you've read any scriptures. It's really quite a unique experience. What ye see isn't happening—it's only a vision ye are having while ye sleep. Unlike most of your dreams, ye don't play a role in it. You're just an observer."

Joe led Kirk to a table at the center of the bar where a lot of action seemed to be taking place. Several people were gathered around the table. Two of the men were having a chugging contest. Both of them appeared to be doing well at putting the drinks away, but their drunkenness showed in their eyes. One of the men, a muscular fellow with a large mustache, slammed his empty glass down as he finished the last round the fastest.

"I need to go home," slurred the man as he stood up, nearly falling to the ground.

"You better let me give you a ride, Kevin," said one of the other men in the group as several exchanged knowing glances about his drunken state.

"I'm fine," he replied with a note of irritation in his voice.

The man who offered the ride shrugged his shoulders and walked to the bar for another round.

"Let's go see how Kevin does, shall we, lad?"

Kirk glanced at the clock behind the bar.

11:55. I guess he's going to turn into a pumpkin if he doesn't leave before midnight, Kirk joked to himself.

Kirk and Joe followed Kevin out of the bar.

"I don't need a ride home," said Kevin in an irritated tone, slamming his hand down hard on the trunk of the blue Monte Carlo parked in front of the bar.

A yellow cat that had been sleeping in the fender well of the car shot out from underneath, running into Kevin's leg.

"Holy sh—" Kevin jumped in the air but failed to complete a perfect landing in his drunken state.

Kirk laughed at the sight.

Kevin stood up, regained his composure, and made his way toward an older model Ford pickup with a tool rack on the back.

"Let's go for a ride, lad."

Kirk found himself in the middle of the bench seat of the truck, with Kevin on his left and Joe on his right. Kirk wasn't sure he would get use to this "dream mission thing" Joe was taking him on.

Kevin shifted into drive and accelerated. His eyes looked as though he was ready to pass out behind the wheel.

"This guy shouldn't be driving," stated Kirk.

"I agree, lad."

Kevin sped down the street crossing back and forth over the centerline during periods of dozing off. The truck bounced as it hit the curb on the side of the street.

"Whoa," Kevin murmured as he pulled back into his lane. "Wake up, man. Only a few more blocks . . . you can do it," he urged to himself.

"PULL OVER, MAN! COME ON!" Kirk yelled, consumed by the situation, forgetting it was only a vision.

The truck sped up, as if going faster would get him there before he had a chance to doze off.

Kirk looked at the speedometer. *Fifty-two miles an hour. He's gonna kill someone!*

They sped toward an intersection with a red light.

"Kirk, I would like to introduce ye to the Jones family."

Kirk saw the car coming through the intersection from the right.

He's not even looking. There's no way he's gonna see them.

"STOP!" yelled Kirk.

Kirk could see the surprised look from the man in the driver's seat of the car as he first noticed the oncoming pickup truck. He also noticed a figure in the passenger seat. What caught his attention most was the kid in the back seat looking out the window. A look of complete horror came to his face as he noticed the pickup speeding towards them.

The sound of glass breaking and metal bending filled the air. Kirk found himself on the sidewalk watching the rest of the wreck happen from a less involved position.

"Ed and Linda Jones and their nine-year-old boy, Jeff. Just back from vacation in Florida. Linda wanted to stop in Oklahoma for the night, but Ed decided to save a little money on hotels and drive on through. A decision he likely will regret when he thinks back on it, lad."

"That means he's going to be all right?" asked Kirk as he found a little hope in the horrible scene he had witnessed.

"Ed and Linda will make it after a few days in the hospital," Joe replied. "What about the kid?"

Joe said no words, but he could see the answer in his solemn reaction.

"NO! God, no!" Kirk looked into what was left of the red car.

Linda made a small moaning sound as though she was just losing consciousness. Her face had cuts from where she hit the dashboard. Ed was conscious, but his actions showed he was in pain.

"Jeff," he said, trying to turn, but his body would not allow the movement in his injured condition. "Are you okay, buddy? JEFF?" he begged frantically. No response.

Kirk looked in the back seat. His mind told him he did not want to see it, but he was compelled to look. The small body lay motionless in the floorboard of the car. The pickup had hit the rear door of the car on the same side Jeff had been sitting. His body lay motionless, but to Kirk he did not look injured minus a small cut on his forehead.

"NO!" said Kirk as the senselessness of the situation overwhelmed him.

"WHY DID YOU DO THAT?" Kirk shouted as he walked toward the pickup truck.

Kevin sat in the truck with blood running down his face, murmuring inaudibly. Kirk tried to reach in and grab him and shake some sense into him. His inability to touch him only fueled the anger he was feeling.

"YOU STUPID DRUNK BASTARD! Look what you've done. LOOK!"

The words had no effect on him.

"He's not going to hear you, lad."

Kirk turned around with tears running down his cheeks.

"This is senseless. Why does this happen?"

This is too much like the night Sarah died. It's like living my nightmare all over again.

Kirk sat on the curb and began to sob uncontrollably. When he was done, he raised his head to find himself sitting on the floor in a strange apartment face to face with Kevin who was also sobbing uncontrollably. His face was not as clean shaven as it had been at the bar.

I remember looking like that. He's losing it.

Kirk, seconds ago at the crash site, bitterly despised Kevin for the terrible accident he had caused. Now in his apartment, seeing this man broken down, hurting from the pain he had caused, Kirk saw himself in Kevin, years ago after his accident. Not something he was proud of, but he understood. Kevin's thoughtless actions had caused more hurt than he could stand.

"Is this what's going to happen after the wreck?"

"He's not going to make it, lad. The guilt's going to be too much for him to handle, and he's going to take his own life. Remember, ye have the ability to stop it."

Kirk stood up and looked thoughtfully at the picture above Kevin.

Reminds me of the one grandpa had. Old bird dog with a quail in his mouth and red barn in the background. Hope you can help me with this, Grandpa, thought Kirk.

"I have to do more than just stop the wreck, don't I?"

"Yes. Even if this wreck is stopped, there will be others. Kevin's on a path destined for destruction. Just like ye were, lad. Ye have to show him how to get off that path, convince him there's a better way."

"This can't happen," said Kirk in a determined tone. "I'm gonna do whatever it takes to stop it. I have to."

CHAPTER 46

Kirk awoke as the sun was setting. He had slept through most of the day.

Looks like I'll be traveling to Texas, he thought to himself as he jumped out of bed and put on his clothes.

Kirk decided to make himself, Larry, and Ron something to eat before they headed out.

I wonder if Ron's going with me or not.

*   *   *

"Hope you're making enough for four people. I'm hungry enough for two," declared Ron as he walked into the kitchen.

"Morning, Ron. Did you sleep okay?"

Ron gave him a strange look. His hair stuck up nearly a half a foot above his head from sleeping on it.

"Nice hair," commented Kirk with a grin.

"Had a dream," muttered Ron apprehensively.

"Me too. Said I needed to head to Texas. What about you?" asked Kirk, hoping they would not have to split up yet.

"I'm going to New Jersey. Supposed to ride up there with some guy who's going to stop by here this evening. Strange thing is the guy I'm going up there to help has the same problem I had."

"Me too. I think part of the redemption is to keep someone from making the same mistakes we made."

"Do you think you can stop him?" Ron asked after exchanging stories.

He seems to have the same doubts in his own abilities that I have in mine.

"I have to," replied Kirk. "There's too much to lose if I don't. After receiving my vision, I'm convinced this Order is taken care of by higher powers. We wouldn't be given something we can't do."

"I hope you're right."

CHAPTER 47

Kirk pulled off the main highway onto the blacktop road that ran through the town of Lakebend, Kansas. The church sat in the northwest corner of the intersection of South Street and Highway 36. The church appeared to no longer be in use. The brick building had eight arched windows on the north side. Broken concrete steps led up into the building. Each of the arched windows were matched up with a perfectly square window directly below, near the ground level of the building.

The main entrance at the front of the church was a large double door with small glass panes framed in directly above the door and a larger arched window centered higher above with two smaller arched windows at either side. The brick façade rose up above the tinned roof and stair stepped up to the final height that was pitched directly above the width of the entrance way. Two flights of concrete steps with a flat concrete pad between them led to the entrance.

Just like the lady said it would be.

Kirk had stopped for fuel near the South Dakota–Nebraska state line and was approached by a woman that he estimated to be in her late twenties.

"It's been a while since you've been to confession," she stated.

Kirk held his head down.

"I know you've been avoiding it," she continued. "Holding in your emotions . . . not wishing to let anyone inside your head . . . but you need this. Before you continue on your mission, this needs to happen. I know a place. It's on your way to Texas. The church will be unlocked. There will be someone in the confessional when you get there."

Kirk got out of his car and walked up the first flight of stairs.

You've got to do this! As much as you've avoided talking about it to friends, priests, and psychologists, the lady was right. You need to get yourself right before you can help others.

Kirk walked up the second flight of stairs and grabbed the door handle, not certain if it would be unlocked. He pulled it open with ease.

"She was right about it being open. Now I just have to see if someone is in the confessional."

Kirk walked in. The south side of the church had eight arched windows matching the north side. Everything in the church was covered in a thin layer of dust. It was as though everyone left church one day and just never returned.

Strange, thought Kirk.

On the south side of the church, Kirk noticed the confessional. It was like the ones he had seen in movies at the larger churches in big cities. The dark, hand-crafted woodwork was impressive. The confessional rose to within five feet of the twenty-foot-tall ceiling with a dark wooden crucifix centered on the top. It had one large wooden door in the center of what Kirk estimated to be a six-foot-deep by fifteen-foot-wide structure.

Seems like I'm always in the confessional, thought Kirk as he pulled open the door.

Kirk was momentarily blind as he stepped from the window-lit interior of the church into the dark confessional room.

"Close the door!" The voice startled Kirk.

Kirk squinted to see where the voice came from on the right side of the room.

"Are you here for confession?" asked Kirk.

"I'll hear your sins."

Kirk turned and closed the door.

As his eyes adjusted to the darkness, he could make out a form of who he assumed to be the priest sitting on the right side of the confessional.

"Sit," commanded the voice.

Kirk reached out and felt a chair on the left side of the room. He sat down.

"It's been a while since you've had a confession, hasn't it, Kirk?"

He knows my name! His voice sounds familiar. Where have I heard it before?

"It's been awhile," Kirk answered hesitantly, still trying to place the familiar voice.

"Go ahead with your confession."

"Well, I assume since you know my name you must know at least some of my story. I used to drink a lot. It got to be a real problem. I . . . I . . . well, I ended up drinking and driving and killed my girlfriend. I haven't forgiven myself yet, and now I've been sent on a mission to stop someone from doing the same thing I did and I'm not sure I can."

Kirk hesitated, waiting for the priest to reply.

"I doubt you can."

"What…what…?" It was the only thing he could get out of his mouth at the unexpected response.

"I'm here to make sure you don't," the man said as candles placed around the room suddenly lit.

"I become stronger and harder to fight as you get older!" expressed the man as Kirk was suddenly able to see his face.

"The dragon!" Kirk exclaimed, suddenly realizing why the voice was familiar. "The…dragon from my dream. You have his voice."

Kirk jumped up and took a step back, falling into the wall of the confessional.

"Oh, it's my voice," said the dark-haired man, smiling. He stood over Kirk. He was tall, and dressed in an expensive, tailored suit. His brown eyes glowed.

"Would you care for a drink?" The man walked over to a table behind where he had been sitting. The gold trimmed table was stocked with liquor.

I must be having another vision, thought Kirk. *I really think I'm here, though. I don't remember going to sleep. I drove straight from Indemnity. I'm here. No vision, no dream.*

"Are you…are you Satan?" asked Kirk.

"Yes. Would you like that drink?"

"No. I just need to get out of here."

"The drink I can give you. Getting out of here is something I won't allow, at least not until it's too late to complete your mission."

"So the lady that told me to come here…"

"She works for my side…the organization that is the opposite of The Order. My team, so to speak," said Satan as he poured bourbon into a small glass. "It's our job to make sure you don't complete the mission. I need for Kevin to kill that boy." Satan continued, "I need for you to fail. All the hate towards Kevin for his mistake. All the guilt from you and him. My side wins. Tips the balance in my favor. The world is a little more…a little more ME." Satan grinned.

"How can you even be in here?" challenged Kirk. "This is God's place."

"How can I not be here?" countered Satan. "In this confessional? This is where people come to get rid of me. At least get rid of the side effects of me. The guilt, the pain. Boo hoo, I sinned, and now I have to deal with the consequences. Forgive me," he mocked.

"I don't always win in this room, but it wouldn't need to be here if it wasn't for me. A lot of people leave me here, for a while. They usually find a way back to me."

Kirk tried to shake his thoughts free of fear. He needed to find a way out.

"You just have to ride out the next few days. Today is Wednesday. If I keep you here until Friday morning, you don't stand a chance at completing your mission. You might as well enjoy a drink. It will make the time pass quicker."

Kirk ignored the offer. "I just have to walk out of this room. I will fight to get through you. The last time I fought you I won."

"No. The time you fought me in a dream, years ago, you won. I won the night you killed Sarah. I've been winning every day since then."

"Until the Order intervened," Kirk pointed out.

Satan's eyes flashed with anger. His controlled composure that he held up to this point was gone. "I have you, Kirk. You are not leaving here until I say so. You're mine."

I can't let him win.

"I'm walking out."

Kirk reached for the door handle. He turned to see what Satan would do.

He smiled. "I won't stop you. That's not my job." He said, taking a drink.

Kirk stepped out the door. In the church semi-circled around the confessional stood five demons. They had a basic human form, but their skin was more like a reptile. Had they been standing fulling erect they would be nearly six feet tall. Their teeth seemed to be outside their head with no lips to cover them. Out of their backs were bat-like wings that spanned nearly ten feet.

"It's THEIR job to keep you here," revealed Satan with a smile.

Kirk estimated the distance from where he stood to the door was thirty feet. Forty or more by the time he ran around the pews. One of the demons stood directly in that path.

If their wings work, I doubt I just have to get through one of them. GO NOW!

Kirk ran for the back of the church. He saw the demon that was in his path growl and tense up, readying himself to stop him. The others took to the air. They were on him before he made it to the back of the church. The first one from the air knocked him down, and the rest of them piled on. Their fists hit Kirk hard. He could only hold his arms up and deflect some of the blows.

Fight, Kirk thought. *You have to get out of here.*

The attack seemed to go on forever. When it finally ended, Kirk lay on the ground.

"Ohhhh." Kirk slowly moved.

"Don't move toward the door, and they won't attack," Satan informed Kirk.

"It's a hard lesson I have to teach people who try to leave," he continued. "A lesson that Cade Remington learned and accepted."

"Who is Cade Remington?" moaned Kirk as he lay on the ground not moving.

Wow. I've never hurt like this. Pretty sure I have a broken rib. I can feel blood dripping down my face.

"Cade Remington, twenty-three years old, Westville, Ohio. The Order tasked him with stopping a young man from drinking and taking his girlfriend on a ride that ended her life. He had a similar sin that he was hoping to be redeemed from. He failed you, Kirk. He failed himself, and he failed The Order. I won."

"He didn't fail me. I failed me. That's not fair to him. If he had saved me, good for him. He can't be held accountable for what I did. I will get out of here. I will save Kevin." Kirk knew he didn't sound as convincing as he hoped.

I'm getting out of here, though I'm not really sure how right now, thought Kirk as he passed out from the pain.

CHAPTER 48

"Ohhh." Kirk's eyes opened to the sunlight coming in one of the smaller windows on the east side of the church. He took a deep breath. "Maybe my ribs aren't broken. Hurts bad, though."

Kirk slowly stood. The demons were all perched on top of pews spread out through the church. Eyes fixed on Kirk, muscles tense, ready for him to move towards the door at the back of the church.

No sign of Satan. I don't think I'm ready to fight those guys yet, thought Kirk as he looked at the demons. *Got to figure out a strategy. I guess if I want to figure this out and get to Kevin in time, I need to go talk to him. Maybe I need to go back to the confessional. It did hurt a little to hear that Cade Remington couldn't fight through this to save me. Not his fault, but I can't do that to the Jones family and Kevin or put myself through the failure if I don't succeed. It's just more guilt if I don't.*

Kirk walked into the confessional.

"Ready for that drink yet?" asked Satan, lifting his glass to Kirk.

Man, that sounds good. Might make some of this pain go away. Don't acknowledge the question.

"What's it take to get out of here?"

"I don't have a price for that. I'm better paid if you don't get out of here. Might as well accept the fact that you aren't going anywhere. It will be a lot easier if you accept it."

"I've learned that the easy road is not always the best."

Kirk jumped at Satan. His hands wrapped around his neck.

"I WON'T ACCEPT IT!" Kirk exclaimed.

Kirk squeezed his hands together tightly around Satan's neck.

Kirk seemed to have little effect on him as he squeezed tighter.

"Trying to kill me is the same as trying to escape. They have my back."

Kirk felt hands grab his body and pull him out of the confessional. He screamed as he was yanked nearly fifteen feet in the air as one of the demons flew him out of the confessional and into the main area of the church.

The demon dropped him into the pews. As he fell, the back of his head hit the pew, knocking him unconscious.

CHAPTER 49

"Wake up, lad. Wake up."

"Hmmmm."

"Wake up, Kirk."

"Joe?"

"Yes. It's Joe, lad."

"Finally, a vision. I guess it's a vision. I'm not so sure anymore. What was that at the church in Lakebend?"

"This is a vision. That's not. That's real, lad. It's life or death, for the Jones family and for Kevin."

I've never seen Joe look this serious.

"Ye have to get out of there, Kirk! Finish the mission. The balance tips to their favor if ye don't. Your faith has to be strong."

"But I've tried, Joe. They're too strong. I'm no match for them. Did you see what they did to me? I CAN'T COMPETE WITH THEM!" Kirk exclaimed with a sense of frustration.

"You got to remember how you beat him in your dream, lad."

"That was a dream, Joe. I beat him in a dream."

"Ye forgot, lad. Ye forgot your strength."

"The sword?" asked Kirk.

Joe looked at Kirk sympathetically. "No. Your strength. Close your eyes, Kirk."

Kirk closed his eyes.

"Think back to the dream, Kirk. To the part right before you killed the dragon."

Kirk played the dream in his mind. The confessional exploded. The dragon. The dragon stood over him…

"You may be able to fight temptation now, but as you grow older, I grow stronger and harder to defeat."

A vision of Jesus being with him at that time came to him. Kirk had forgotten that part of the dream.

It was Jesus that brought me through.

I fell to the ground when the dragon burst out of the room.

"Don't be afraid. I will be your strength," said Jesus, reaching his hand out to lift him off the ground.

"I did see him, Joe. I saw him for just long enough to realize he was there to help me. It did give me the courage and the strength to defeat the dragon."

"Remember the faith you had in God back then. Remember the feeling you had when you defeated the dragon. That will pull you through."

CHAPTER 50

The demons sat on the top of the back row of pews evenly spaced across them. Their wings tucked close to their bodies. Their eyes ever alert, focused on Kirk, waiting for any movement towards the back of the church.

Kirk lay asleep, on the floor between the pews. They had watched him through the better part of the day. The sun was now shining from the west through the most westerly window on the south side of the church.

A slight moan came from Kirk as his body slowly and painfully began to move.

"Ohhh." Kirk grabbed the back of his head. His eyes opened, but only after some effort.

Where am I?

Kirk stood up.

He turned to the back of the church. A moment of fear as he saw the demons.

Oh, yeah. Lakebend, at the church. Need to get out of here.

Kirk noticed the sun at the southwest corner of the church.

Thursday evening. Unless I was unconscious longer. Could it be Friday evening? I don't know.

"I see you're awake, Kirk," remarked Satan as he came out of the confessional. "You might as well sit down and relax. You gave it a good effort, though you didn't stand a chance."

NO. No. I haven't given it a good effort. He's still trying to keep me from trying. I'm saying it is Thursday evening. I still have time. What do I need to do?

Kirk ignored Satan and began to walk to the front of the church.

"It's over, Kirk. Don't be a fool. Look at them!" Satan grabbed Kirk and turned him to face the demons.

"You have to get through them and out that door."

Why is he trying to get me to focus on the back of the church when I was heading to the front? He doesn't want me to go to the front of the church.

Kirk turned and hurriedly ran toward the sanctuary.

"Stop him!" shouted Satan.

The demons rapidly took to the air. Kirk was almost to the first step of the sanctuary when one of the demons knocked him to the ground. Kirk quickly stood and lunged forward. One of the demons narrowly missed Kirk as he fell down on the sanctuary. He turned to face what he was sure would be another attack.

The demons and Satan stood at the bottom step of the sanctuary. Kirk waited for the attack . . . it never came.

What . . . what is going on here? First, they didn't want me out the back door, then they try to attack me for coming up on the sanctuary. Now they are just staring at me.

"You can't come up here, can you?" said Kirk with a smile.

Satan's jaw stiffened.

"You still have to get out the back door."

He turned and walked away. The demons, one by one, flew to the back of the church, taking their previous guarding positions.

That was strange, thought Kirk with amazement. *There's something up here they don't want me to see...or have.*

Kirk looked around the sanctuary. The tabernacle where the communion was kept was open and empty. Nothing on the altar.

What's up here?

Kirk walked to the pulpit.

The hardbound book with the readings for each weekend was laying closed on top of the pulpit.

Three ribbons to mark the pages for the weekend's readings were placed throughout the book at varying locations.

The word of God, Kirk thought as he ran his hand over the front of the book.

Speak to me, Lord…show me the way. I have to get out of here and help Kevin…and the Jones family. Don't let me fail. Please, God.

Kirk opened the book to the first marked reading. He stood at the pulpit looking out over the pews.

"A reading from the book of Second Samuel," Kirk read aloud.

"STOP!" shouted Satan, bursting out of the door of the confessional.

The demons left their perch with a loud scream and began to circle the area of the church above the pews.

Kirk continued.

The Lord thundered from heaven; the Most High gave forth his voice. He sent forth arrows to put them to flight; he flashed lightning and routed them. Then the well springs of the sea appeared, the foundations of the earth were laid bare, at the rebuke of the Lord, at the blast of the wind of his wrath.

He reached out from on high and grasped me; he drew me out of the deep waters. He rescued me from my mighty enemy, from my foes, who were too powerful for me. They attacked me on the day of calamity, but the Lord came to my support. He set me free in the open, and rescued me, because he loves me.

Kirk looked up. The demons began to scream again. Satan cursed aloud.

Kirk felt a wave of courage as he read.

Did they stop the screaming while I was reading? I couldn't hear them. It seems to be upsetting them. Read the next one.

Kirk opened the book to the next marked section. His trembling hands were barely able to turn the pages.

Kirk continued.

A reading from the letter to the Ephesians.

Kirk paused. He looked up to see Satan. He had transformed from a man to a large, man-like, horned beast. He stood as near the sanctuary as possible.

"YOU WON'T SUCCEED, KIRK. YOU KILLED SARAH! REMEMBER KILLING SARAH."

The demons were tearing the church apart. Pews were hurled across the church. Smashing as they were thrown against walls and columns.

Stay strong. Keep your faith. YOU WILL NOT FAIL, Kirk thought, trying to bring himself encouragement. Kirk looked down at the book and continued.

Finally draw your strength from the Lord and from his mighty power. Put on the armor of God so that you may be able to stand firm against the tactics of the devil. For our struggle is not with flesh and blood but with the principalities, with the powers, with the world rulers of this present darkness, with the evil spirits in the heavens. Therefore, put on the armor of God, that you may be able to resist on the evil day and having done everything, to hold your ground. So stand fast with your loins girded in truth, clothed with righteousness as a breastplate, and your feet shod in readiness for the gospel of peace. In all circumstances, hold faith as a shield, to quench all flaming arrows of the evil one. And take the helmet of salvation and the sword of the spirit, which is the Word of God.

Kirk felt a hand on his shoulder.

"I'm with you, Kirk. Go now."

Kirk turned, but no one was there. He knew it was God. A surge of strength flooded him. "He's with me!" said Kirk out loud.

A feeling that he could accomplish anything as long as he kept his faith came over Kirk. God was with him.

Kirk read the last line back to himself.

"And take the helmet of salvation and the sword of the Spirit, which is the word of God."

Take the book with you.

Kirk turned the book to the final marked page. He looked up. Kirk had not seen him leave, but Satan was gone. The demons remained. Their rampage continued as they destroyed the inside of the church.

He grabbed the book, held it in front of him, and slowly began to walk to the back of the church.

"A reading from the Book of Psalms," Kirk began to read. "The Lord is my shepherd; I shall not want. He makes me to lie down in green pastures; he leads me beside the still waters. He restores my soul; He leads me in the path of righteousness for his name's sake."

Kirk looked up from the book. The demons had all moved in front of the back door. All standing shoulder to shoulder, creating a wall between the exit and Kirk. Their breathing was heavy from the physical energy they had exerted during their rampage.

Kirk smiled. He once again felt the hand on his shoulder.

"I know you're with me," he said.

He set the book down in one of the pews that remained in place and continued from memory.

"Yea, though I walk through the valley of the shadow of death, I will fear no evil: For you are with me; with thy rod and staff that give me comfort and courage."

Kirk ran towards the demons. They tensed and lowered themselves, preparing for the hit.

The demons seemed weaker than before. Kirk's momentum took them out through the back door. He felt them grabbing and punching as they tried to hold him in the church. Instead, they all fell out onto the landing in the middle of the stairs. The demons faced Kirk and growled at him before flying away.

Kirk watched them fly off to the north.

"I did it! YES. I DID IT!"

Kirk jumped down the bottom flight of stairs.

Kirk smiled.

"I mean WE did it. Thank you, God. Thank you!"

CHAPTER 51

Kirk pulled into a small convenience store in Shoresburg, Oklahoma.

4:15 Friday morning. Should be enough time to get to Elam, he thought to himself.

He had left Lakebend at around 11:00 p.m. He was preparing to stop for a couple of hours, catch a nap, fill up with gas, and get something to eat. He estimated this tank of gas was going to take him all the way to Elam, but he had a growing concern in the back of his mind about how he would eat for the rest of the time he was on this mission and how he was going to make it back to Washington with his limited money supply.

I'll just stay focused on what I need to do in Elam, he thought to himself. The trip so far had been consumed with trying to come up with ideas for stopping Kevin from destroying his life.

Hope it comes to me soon. Hey, I haven't thought about my own guilt this whole trip. Guess I'm too worried about someone else's trouble to be thinking about my own. I like this. I finally learned to start liking myself when I put others' needs before my own.

Kirk remembered Larry saying that before he left. The words didn't mean much to him at the time, but now he was able to start understanding the process of forgiving himself.

Kirk pulled up to the gas tank. As he stepped out of the car, he checked the contents of his wallet to ensure he had enough to pay for the gas.

$56 left. Takes about $25 to fill up. Wished I had known I was going to take this side trip when I pulled my money out of the bank.

"You heading to Texas?"

Kirk spun around to see a man in a suit jacket wearing a cowboy hat.

"Going to Elam," replied Kirk uncertain as to where this conversation was going.

"Nick Norton," said the man, giving Kirk a broad smile that displayed his dimples and nearly perfect teeth.

"Kirk Murphy."

Nick grabbed Kirk's hand and shook it vigorously.

"When you finish filling up, I'm supposed to pay for your gas and buy you some dinner."

"Why would you do that?" asked Kirk.

"I was told if I took care of that you would give me a ride to my home in Houston."

"That's a deal," said Kirk as a few of the financial questions in his head were answered.

The Lord will provide, thought Kirk to himself as he followed Nick into the store.

"Get whatever you need to eat," said Nick.

CHAPTER 52

Kirk discovered from his ride with Nick to Houston that he had been a stockbroker who embezzled his clients' money. "You know," Nick said, "I didn't realize how much my conscience was bothering me until I started doing good for people. I took away all those years selfishly, thinking I would be happy with the money, but until I gave to someone else, I was so unhappy."

"How come you need a ride to Houston?" asked Kirk, wondering why a man who had money would not be driving.

"I gave my car away," said Nick laughing. "Can you believe it? I just gave it away. It wasn't even part of my mission. I just saw a lady with two kids broke down on the side of the road. Turns out she was a single mom and couldn't afford to even have the broken-down car fixed. I gave her the car and some money to take care of bills. I don't think I ever made anyone that happy in my entire life. I wasn't worried about how I would make it home. I only knew it felt good to help. Better than I've felt in a long time." Nick was almost glowing as he explained how good he felt about himself.

"Now what?" asked Kirk.

"I have enough money to invest and make a lot of money off the earnings to help a lot of people and to help The Order out when such a time comes and I've been told it will."

"I can take the first shift of driving if you would like. You look a little beat up and tired, if you don't mind my saying so," said Nick.

"I'll take you up on that," replied Kirk.

I am feeling a whole lot of soreness from the demon attack. I could use a couple hours of sleep.

CHAPTER 53

Kirk looked up to find himself in the church at Lansing, Missouri.

Must be another vision. Oh, yeah. I'm on my way to Texas. Nick is driving.

"Hello, Kirk," said Joe as he stepped out of the confessional.

Kirk made a slight jerking motion as he was startled by the silence being broken.

"Do you like to scare me like that?" asked Kirk with a smile.

"It does give me a little pleasure," said Joe smiling. "Ye seem to have a lot of questions in your mind, and I was free, so I thought ye may need someone to talk to. That's part of the problem with people in the world—they like to lock up their feelings inside and don't talk to their loved ones about what's bothering them. That causes the problem to become worse. So why don't ye try telling me what's on yer mind, lad." Joe sat down next to Kirk.

Kirk took a deep breath. He had always bottled up his feelings inside and would not talk to anyone. Now here was someone that knew exactly what he was thinking and would not allow him the luxury of not talking about it.

"How come you know what I'm thinking, but you want me to tell you?" asked Kirk.

"It was never intended for ye to have someone know what ye were thinking. Ye were given the gift of speech so ye didn't have to hold your thoughts and feelings in. Your whole life you've never used this gift to its full capacity."

The words fell like a load of bricks on Kirk. Here was someone God sent to deliver messages telling him he had wasted a gift he had been given. Joe remained silent as though waiting for a reply. Kirk remained silent, mulling over this new wisdom.

"I know what you're thinking," said Joe. "It should be easy to tell me. You'll be surprised how good ye will feel about getting your fears out in the open."

"I'M SCARED." The words Kirk had been telling himself in his mind were finally on his lips. "I don't think I can do what you're asking me. Part of me is determined to go to Elam and stop this guy, save his life, and the kid's life. I don't want him to go through what I had to go through. Another part of me is terrified. What if I don't stop him? What can I say that will stop him? In my mind I can see what needs to be done, but I know it's going to be so much harder to do when I'm there. I keep questioning how I'm going to stop it. What if I can't stop it? Can I live with the guilt of their deaths on my shoulders because I couldn't?" Kirk took a deep breath. The words he had been holding in his mind, that kept repeating themselves because he would not set them free through his spoken words, were now released along with some of the fear he had been holding inside.

Joe smiled. "Now there's the way ye need to use that gift. Let it out. It doesn't do anything inside ye except give ye doubt and worry. There is one more concern about the guilt ye may feel if you're not successful that ye may want to talk to me about."

"You mean I'll feel guiltier about not succeeding if I don't try?"

"You've done a wonderful job saying exactly what's on your mind. If ye can do that with Kevin, ye won't have anything to feel guilty about." Joe stood up and walked out of the church.

Kirk sat in the silence of the church. For the first time since he found out about Kevin, he was able to enjoy the silence without the thoughts in his head making him doubt what he could, or could not, do.

Should have talked to someone about that a long time ago, thought Kirk.

CHAPTER 54

Kevin Lampkin pulled up to the house his company had been hired to build at the Sunrise Acres subdivision. Several men were on the roof putting shingles into place, while other hammers could be heard inside the home.

"Morning, Bill," said Kevin with a grin that made his black mustache tilt up on the left side of his otherwise boyish face.

"Damn it, Kevin, this is the third time this month you've been late and I don't even want to hear an excuse because I'm tired of hearing 'em. If I wasn't short of good help, I would send you packing. You smell like a keg of beer. This is your last chance, Kevin. You get in that truck, go home, sleep it off, and come back Monday sobered up and we'll talk," scolded Bill.

Kevin, without a word, headed back to the driver's side of the truck Bill lent him to get to work.

"What the hell did you do to my truck?" Bill said, noticing a new dent in the front fender.

"Someone hit me in the parking lot at the grocery store after I left work yesterday," said Kevin, hoping he sounded convincing.

"If I so much as find out you drove my truck drunk and hit something, you're out of here. I don't care how good a worker you are. You need to get your damn fool head on straight before you screw up royal. Now go home and come back on Monday . . . sober." Bill turned, shaking his head as though he still had plenty to say but didn't have the time to waste on it.

"GET THE HELL BACK TO WORK!" Bill shouted, noticing work on the site had come to a halt while everyone stopped to watch the exchange.

Kevin knew he was furious because they had fallen behind schedule and Bill had them working five, twelve-hour days a week and was threatening to start working Saturday if they couldn't catch up.

I could go sleep it off like Bill said, but hell I slept from 1:00 last night until 9:00 this morning. It is Friday and since I have the day off and it's almost noon I think I'm going to start partying a little early today. Hell, I can slow down on Monday when I HAVE to be back at work. Besides, everyone's going to be at Steve's Place tonight.

Kevin pulled into the liquor store to pick up a case of beer.

CHAPTER 55

Kirk stood outside the bar at Elam, Texas. He had dropped Nick off in Houston and finished the drive to Elam. He made it with only two hours to spare.

He took a deep breath as he entered the smoke and chaos inside Steve's Place. He was still uncertain as to what he would say or do to convince Kevin not to get behind the wheel, but he was determined to stop him.

The bar was filled with loud music from a DJ. Kirk could barely make out how much he needed to pay for a cover charge. He handed the lady at the entrance $10 and waited to see if she asked for more or gave him back change. She handed him a $5 bill.

"Thank you," he said, doubting she heard him. A smile was her only reply. Kirk waded through the crowd towards the bar.

Which table were they? thought Kirk, trying to remember from his vision where he had seen Kevin and his friends. Kirk looked around only to see a different group of people sitting at the table than the ones he had seen in his vision.

Must not be here yet, Kirk thought to himself as he ordered a cup of coffee from a bartender who looked disgusted at the thought of brewing a pot of coffee.

Kirk ignored the look but found comfort in the fact that the coffee would be fresh. He had enough four- and five-hour-old coffee to know how bad it could taste.

Kirk turned to see Kevin and the crowd he was with entering the bar. From the looks of things, they were some of the regulars at this establishment. The lady taking money waved them in with a friendly hello. Kirk saw her shake her head no as she allowed them in at no charge. The group seemed to liven up the whole atmosphere of the bar.

Their first round was bought by a gentleman at the end of the bar who looked quite natural sitting in that particular seat. *Must be another regular,* thought Kirk to himself.

Kirk looked at the time. 10:25. It would be an hour and a half before Kevin would leave.

Better approach him now while he's not as drunk as he's going to be, thought Kirk, taking a deep breath.

He made his way through the crowd towards the table where the drinking contest was already beginning.

"I need to talk to you," shouted Kirk into Kevin's ear.

"Do I know you?" asked Kevin, beginning to look defensive.

"No," said Kirk. "You look like you've had a lot to drink and I think you should take a taxi home tonight. I'll pay for it." Kirk was a little less than confident about how that was going to be received.

"What are you . . . my mom?" asked Kevin sarcastically. "Leave me alone."

The drunkenness was already obvious in Kevin's eyes.

"No. It's important you don't drive tonight. You have to take a cab or let someone sober drive you. I'll drive you home." Kirk made the offer before he thought about how it would sound.

"Get the hell away from me. I'm not gay," said Kevin as he stood up, knocking his chair over.

"No. No. I'm not trying to pick you up. It's just that—" Kirk stopped himself. *There's no way this guy's gonna believe I had a vision about his wreck.*

"This guy giving you trouble, Kevin?"

Kirk turned to see a large man who must be the bouncer for this bar.

"I think he's trying to pick me up," said Kevin, jerking his head toward the door, which appeared to be the signal for "kick him out."

"Let's go, dude." The bouncer wrapped his giant arm around Kirk's neck and held one arm with his other hand. The pressure around his neck made it difficult to breathe.

"I'll make a bet with you," gasped Kirk.

The bouncer stopped for a minute and looked at Kevin. Kevin's curiosity perked up.

"This better be good," replied Kevin, tensing up as though he was going to hit Kirk at the first sign of some obscene remark.

"If you get knocked down by a cat tonight, you either take a cab home or let me drive you home."

"What do I get if I don't get knocked down by a cat?"

"Fifty bucks," said Kirk, wondering how he would make it home if he lost.

"If I make this bet, will you leave me the hell alone?" asked Kevin.

"Until you get knocked down by a cat, you won't see me again."

"You got a deal, doofus."

Kirk felt as though it would be in his best interest not to ask Kevin to shake to "seal the deal."

CHAPTER 56

Kirk decided to wait across the street from the bar. He wanted to see the whole scene play out from a different angle than he had in his vision. *Kind of like seeing the instant replay on television from a different camera angle,* he thought to himself, trying to forget about the serious nature of what he was here for.

Kirk was uncertain that Kevin would be knocked down by the cat the way he was in his vision.

I'm not even sure if what I've already done has changed the outcome of what's going to happen. At least by the time he comes out, he'll be wasted enough I might be able to physically keep him from driving if his friends don't step in, thought Kirk as he decided his best chance was to separate Kevin from his friends.

11:55. Show time, thought Kirk as Kevin stumbled his way out the door. As Kirk had hoped, Kevin tapped the back of the Monte Carlo. The scene was like watching a rerun. He knew what was going to happen. It still made him smile as the cat knocked Kevin to the ground. This time Kirk was able to see the look of surprise on Kevin's face as the cat ran off. Kirk held back a laugh, realizing that the next few minutes would be critical to keeping Kevin from getting behind the wheel.

"Should I drive, or call you a cab?" asked Kirk, trying to use a tone that would not sound sarcastic or arrogant.

Kevin looked up. He had not seen Kirk standing there and had hoped no one witnessed the scene. Kevin's expression changed as the realization of Kirk's prediction coming true sunk in.

"I don't know how the hell you did that, but stay away from me."

"You made a bet you would let me drive you home or call a cab if that happened. You're not going to back out on that bet, are you?" Kirk said, trying to persuade Kevin to honor his bargain.

"Get away from me," said Kevin, pushing past Kirk.

"I was hoping I wouldn't have to do this." Kirk reached back under his shirt and pulled a pistol out that had been tucked into the top of his jeans. Kevin was opening the door to the truck when he turned and started to say something but stopped short when he saw the pistol in his face.

"Get in the truck. NOW!" said Kirk, trying to intimidate Kevin. It seemed to work. Kevin appeared to sober up rather quickly at the sight of a gun in his face.

"NOW SIT OVER THERE, SHUT UP, AND HANDCUFF YOURSELF TO THE DOOR WITH THESE!" Kirk handed Kevin a set of handcuffs he had purchased with the pistol at a pawn shop after he had been kicked out of the bar. He had not even considered needing a pistol until he realized Kevin's friends may jump into the conflict. From the confrontation before he was kicked out of the bar, Kirk knew he didn't stand a chance alone if his friends got involved.

Kevin complied with Kirk's demand.

Kirk was almost shaking when he first pulled the gun out. He was so nervous, but he surprised himself at the authority he heard in his own voice.

"What are you doing?" asked Kevin as he handcuffed himself to the wing window brace on the door.

"I'm going to show you how bad you almost screwed up tonight," said Kirk. "I just stopped you from killing a nine-year-old boy who was just on his way home with his family." Kirk pulled the truck down the road.

"Slow down, man," said Kevin with a little fear in his voice.

The adrenaline must be sobering him up, thought Kirk as he remembered Kevin barely able to keep his eyes open on this trip. He was driving fast to ensure he made it in time to see the Jones family come through the intersection.

"Now pay attention, Kevin," demanded Kirk as he parked in view of the intersection.

Kevin was beginning to nod off.

Adrenaline must be wearing off, thought Kirk.

"Wake up, Kevin." Kevin's eyes were open, but he was beginning to look sleepy.

"In a minute, a red Plymouth is going to come through this intersection. I want you to look in the back seat at the little kid looking out the window. If I had let you drive tonight, you would have hit the car as it came through the intersection and he would have died."

"How the hell do you know that?" asked Kevin.

"The same way I knew you would get knocked down by a cat. Now watch . . . they should be coming through any second." Kirk barely got the words out when the red Plymouth came through the intersection.

Jeff was looking out the back window. His eyes caught Kevin looking right at him. Jeff raised his hand slowly as if to wave, but no smile came to his face. As quickly as they appeared, they were gone.

"Take me home," said Kevin.

Something in his voice changed. Kirk couldn't tell what it was, but something about seeing them cross the intersection got to him.

I hope he's seen enough to change his ways, thought Kirk hopefully.

CHAPTER 57

Ron walked into a pawn shop in Clark, Wisconsin. The man behind the counter wore a white tank top that allowed his large keg-shaped belly to hang out the bottom.

"I have twenty bucks, and I need to buy a video camera," said Ron in a panicked voice.

"Twenty bucks and you can LOOK at all the expensive ones. Thirty and you can touch one of 'em," said the man in a sarcastic tone.

"I need one," demanded Ron, annoyed at the tone of the man's voice.

"Not my problem," he said with a laugh.

"How much to rent one for a few hours?"

"I'm not going to rent one out. What the hell's your problem?"

Ron walked up to the counter with a video camera in hand. "Here's twenty bucks," he said in an angry tone, grabbing the man by the front of his shirt. "Make me out a receipt for three hours' rental, and I will be back in two and a half hours."

The man looked into Ron's eyes and saw no room for negotiation. The man behind the counter was unaccustomed to people being larger than he was, but this man had him by a couple of inches and appeared to be in much better physical condition than he was.

"Alright. I'll rent you the damn camera, just ease up, man."

Ron glared at the man as he made out the receipt for three hours' rental on a video camera. He almost ran out of the store, realizing he was almost out of time.

Three blocks away. He almost ran the whole way.

Ron slowed to a walk as he neared a small alley situated between several old buildings that should have been condemned years before. The alley was littered with empty liquor bottles and newspapers blowing out of a dumpster located about halfway down the alley. He tried to adjust his eyes to the darkness as he walked away from the street lights.

Ron remembered the old creaking fire escape he saw to his left. The bottom section seemed to be hanging on by what appeared to be a small metallic thread. On his right was an old building that had given up some of its bricks and was in danger of losing more.

Let's see, Ron thought to himself, almost sure he was in the right alley. *He was on the other side of the dumpster.*

Ron walked down the alley. He fumbled with the video camera to make sure it was ready to record. The man at the pawn shop also threw in a video tape at Ron's request. As he stepped around the dumpster, he saw a man lying on the pavement injecting himself with heroin.

What a horrible place to be in, thought Ron, trying not to let the putrid smell from the dumpster gag him.

The man looked up, surprised. He had finished the process just as Ron stepped around the corner. "What the hell are you doing?"

The man's eyes had already begun to glaze over.

"Just take it easy," said Ron. "I'm not here to hurt you."

CHAPTER 58

Terrance Clay's eyes opened. The ceiling fan above him was spinning slowly. His mind tried to process how he ended up in a room he was unfamiliar with. Slowly, as though he were under water, he surveyed the room.

In the corner sat a man Terrance was certain he had never seen before in his life.

"Good morning," said the man, allowing Terrance the time to orient himself to his surroundings.

"Hi," said Terrance in an uncertain voice.

"Ron Truitt. Nice to meet you," said Ron, holding his hand out.

Terrance shook hands. "Where am I?"

"You are in a hotel room I'm sure I can't pay for, but I was pretty sure you could."

"Why am I here?" he asked.

"I made a video last night that I'm sure you would like to see," Ron replied.

Ron walked over to the television and hit the play button on the camera he had plugged into it. Terrance sat up in the bed and blinked his eyes to allow himself to better see the television screen. On the screen was a view of an alley. The movement of the camera down the alley was almost enough to give a person motion sickness.

"Hey. This is gonna be a hit at the box office," said Terrance.

"Just watch and shut up," commanded Ron.

The camera moved around the dumpster just in time to see Terrance shooting up.

Terrance watched the film. Seeing himself shooting up beside the dumpster gave him a sick feeling. He remembered from the night before buying the heroin and not wanting to wait until he left the alley to use it.

I can't believe I wanted it that badly, he thought.

"I don't want to see this," he said in an irritated tone, getting up to shut off the television.

"This is you. You can try to deny it all you want, but I have it on film," said Ron. "If you don't watch it, I'm going to make sure your boss and your wife see it."

Terrance looked at Ron. There was absolutely no indication he was bluffing. Terrance was the executive vice president at a local bank and understood that if this tape was released to his boss it would seriously jeopardize his position with the bank. He didn't want to think about the consequences of his wife seeing this, although he was certain she knew he had a drug problem.

"Alright. I'll watch it. Just settle down," said Terrance, afraid this large man was about to lose control.

Ron was focused on this one goal. He knew getting this man to understand how bad his problem was would be the key to stopping him from doing it again. Terrance sat down on the end of the bed. His heart felt heavy at the thought of having to watch the rest of the tape. Terrance saw himself inject the heroin into his arm.

"What the hell are you doing?" Terrance heard himself say.

"Just take it easy. I'm not going to hurt you," said a voice on the tape.

Terrance saw his eyes glaze over as he went into convulsions. His body began to shake. If it had not been himself on the TV, he would have said the man was going to die. Vomit spewed from his mouth. Terrance could not remember any time in his life when he threw up that much.

"I can't believe I look like that."

Ron would not let him turn away.

"You're going to watch every minute of this tape," insisted Ron. "I had to watch the whole thing, and it wasn't pleasant for me. You almost died, and all I could do was film it."

Terrance put his head down in shame.

"Your wife is seriously considering leaving you because of your problem."

"How do you know that?" Terrance asked.

"The same way I knew to film that whole ugly episode last night so you could watch it today. It's out of control." Ron gave Terrance a look that turned an already serious mood into a "this is more serious than you thought" mood.

"I was in your shoes at one time in my life, and it cost me a wife and two kids. I haven't seen them for seven years, and do you want to know what the worst part of it is?" Ron didn't wait for Terrance to answer the question. "The worst part is they are better off without me. Is that what you want? Do you want to look back and realize your wife and kid are better off without you?"

Terrance couldn't think of anything to say.

"You need to get it right, Terrance. Get help."

"I don't know how to quit," said Terrance. The emotion in his voice sounded as though quitting crossed his mind a lot.

"You have to get help. You know it's a problem, and it's time to let your family know you want to get better. Don't be embarrassed to talk to them about getting help because you're going to find out they want you to be the man you used to be. A good dad, husband, and banker. This is your wake-up call. You can ignore this, but it's only going to get worse, if you can imagine what's worse than what you saw on that tape we just watched."

Terrance's eyes were watering. He tried to say something, but the lump in his throat would not allow for speech. He cleared his throat. "Can I have the tape so I can show my wife how bad I am and make sure we want to work through this?"

"You got it," said Ron. "And I'll help you however I can."

CHAPTER 59

Ron pulled up to a small house in Louisburg, Idaho. The yard was fully enclosed with a white picket fence in the front that connected to a chain link fence enclosing the remaining portion of the back yard. The black shutters stood out against the white house. In the front yard on the inside of the picket fence was a small fish pond with a running fountain circled by a stunning array of flowers.

She always had a green thumb, thought Ron. *Too bad she didn't have time to use it back then.*

Ron's hair was cut shorter than it had been since he graduated high school. His face was freshly shaven and his clothes consisted of a nicely pressed collared shirt.

I'm so nervous, he thought to himself.

The house looked better than the way he remembered it from his vision when he saw Nancy's thoughts of where she was going to stay if she left him. The house belonged to a family member who was more than happy to rent it to her at a cheap price if she would "leave that loser."

Ron knew he had a lot of his past to overcome to prove to Nancy and her family he had straightened out his life. His knuckles were turning white as he gripped the flowers he had brought for her. The thought of turning and walking away crossed his mind.

Just ring the doorbell, he thought to himself. *There has to be a reason you saw where she lives.*

The door opened. Ron stood there at a loss for words. He had practiced what he was going to say at this moment for the past six months, but now he couldn't utter a sound.

"Can I help you?"

She doesn't recognize me, thought Ron. It had been a long time since she had seen him well groomed.

"It's me, Nancy."

Nancy looked harder, realizing she must know this man standing at her door with flowers.

"Oh, my . . ." She remained silent for a few seconds, and her face went white, almost as if she was going to pass out.

"Kids, go out and play in the back yard."

"Aww, Mom. We're playing video games."

Ron glanced inside to see two kids he knew were his, though they had grown. He knew he had missed a big portion of life. Their life and his suddenly overwhelmed him as he saw these two children who to the best of Ron's memory would be eight and eleven.

"NOW!" insisted Nancy in a tone that caused the children to jump up and hit the back door almost at a run.

"What the hell do you want, and how did you find me?" asked Nancy after she had regained her composure. "I don't want you around anymore."

Ron was expecting to hear that, but the reality of it had more of an effect on him than he had planned for.

Don't give up, he thought to himself.

"Nancy, I know I put you through a lot and I understand you and the kids were better off without me. It was a rotten way to live. I know I don't deserve it, but I'm asking for a second chance, mostly as a dad. I don't expect you to forgive me. You saw how horrible I had become, but I would like a chance to be involved in their life."

Ron could see the children playing catch in the back yard as he took a seat at the kitchen table. Nancy remained quiet, still in shock that Ron had found them.

"What are they like, Nancy? The kids, I mean." Ron was filled with a sudden sense of curiosity.

Nancy took a deep breath. "Nick acts like you. He hardly knew you, but I see it in him almost every day. He wouldn't hurt anyone on purpose, and he's always looking for ways to make me happy. The way you used to before the drugs."

Nancy paused for a minute, carefully considering the words she would use to describe her other child. "Andrew is a curious child. Always asking questions. He's intelligent, Ron. Can you believe coming from the two of us who had C averages all through school?"

Nancy's eyes were glowing as she talked about her kids. Suddenly the reality of who she was talking to sunk in.

"Why should I let you back in their life?" The question was asked with no emotion.

Ron took a moment to make it come out the way he rehearsed. "For five months now I've been employed at a convenience store in Binesford. I have a whole new focus on life and what makes me happy. I want to be involved with my kids. I know I've failed, Nancy. I've failed you, and I failed them, but if you can give me another chance I can be the dad I was when we tucked Nick in at night, when I used to rock him to sleep. I've been clean since the day you left me. It woke me up. I want it back, though I know I don't deserve it." Ron forced himself not to cry. He had promised himself he would not make Nancy feel sorry for him. "But I want it."

"I'll give you a second chance."

"Thank you . . . I—"

"But first," she said, interrupting him, "I'm going to get to know who you are before I let you near our kids. This Friday night come pick me up at seven. I'll have the kids at a sitter's house. We'll discuss your second chance over dinner."

"It's a date," Ron said, smiling.

"Let's call it dinner for now," she said, trying not to set herself up for disappointment.

"Dinner it is," said Ron as he stood up and walked towards the door.

"And don't be late or the deal's off." Nancy tried to sound strict and not let any feelings of excitement show. "And please be the Ron I used to know," she said under her breath as she watched him walk down the street, whistling a tune.

CHAPTER 60

Kirk placed the empty beer cans from the back of Kevin's truck in a neatly spaced row on the picnic table of the roadside park where he and Kevin had spent the night. Kevin was sitting in the same position in the passenger seat of the truck but was beginning to groan, indicating he was either dreaming or nearing the point where he would awaken.

Kirk stepped back about twenty yards from the cans and took a seated position to allow his elbows to rest on his knees. The door of the truck slowly opened and Kevin stepped out looking somewhat confused at the strange place he found himself in. He spotted Kirk sitting down and began to walk towards him. Kirk raised the pistol and took careful aim at the cans.

"Hold on, man!" shouted Kevin in surprise, holding his ears for what he was sure was about to be a loud report from the pistol.

"Plink." A can fell. Kirk smiled to himself at the noise and what he was sure Kevin was thinking. "Plink" another can fell over.

"You son of a—" Kevin was too dumbfounded to finish the sentence. "You held me hostage with a BB gun."

Kirk's smile grew slightly. "Yeah. They have a seven-day waiting period to buy a real pistol, and I didn't exactly get enough notice to buy one that far in advance."

"What the hell are we doing out here?" asked Kevin.

"I couldn't get you to wake up to tell me where you lived, and I didn't have enough to put us up for the night in a hotel."

"Who are you, and what's your beef with me?" asked Kevin.

"Sorry. I forgot to introduce myself. Kirk Murphy," he said, holding out his hand.

Kevin ignored the introduction.

"You remember much about last night?" asked Kirk.

"I remember you coming in to the bar and saying you were supposed to give me a ride home and betting a cat would knock me down." Kevin gave a thoughtful look as the memory of the cat knocking him down came to him. "How did you know that was going to happen?"

"What else do you remember?" asked Kirk, intentionally avoiding the question for the moment.

"You showed me an intersection where you said I would have killed that little kid in the back of the car."

Kirk couldn't tell if Kevin was hung over or if he was in more of a listening mood than he had been the night before, but he seemed to be considering the notion of what Kirk had told him.

Kirk decided to let him process the information for a minute.

"You wanna try?" asked Kirk, handing him the pistol.

"No thanks."

Kevin ran a hand over his face, looking like a man under a spell and trying to break free.

"Here's the strange thing about that kid you showed me in the red car," Kevin said. "I had a dream about a week ago, and that kid told me I should listen to the person who would point him out."

Kirk took a minute to process what he had heard. *Well, God, you have your hand in all of this, don't you?*

"You avoided the question earlier," said Kevin after a moment of silence. "And if I'm not supposed to know the answer, I can deal with that, but I have to ask again. How did you know what was going to happen last night?"

"I had a vision," Kirk began. "I was in your truck. I watched you drive yourself home after Steve's Place. It was horrible." Kirk said remembering the vision. "You passed out, and the truck kept going faster. Your truck rammed the rear driver-side door . . . the one the kid was sitting next to. His mother was unconscious, and the father couldn't turn around to see his dead son." Kirk took a deep breath, noticing the look of horror on Kevin's face at the details.

Don't hold back the truth, said Kirk to himself as he realized he was getting through to Kevin.

"I had another vision of you, Kevin. I was in your apartment a few months later. The guilt was destroying you. It was too much for you, and you took your own life. You were sitting on the floor in a hallway right below the picture of a bird dog with a quail. Red barn in the background."

"How the...I just bought that last week. I was planning on hanging that in the hallway but haven't yet."

"I was sent here to save you from the wreck last night and to tell you to get your life straightened up before you kill someone or yourself. I have something I want to show you," said Kirk, grabbing his wallet from his back pocket. "This was my girlfriend Sarah. I overdid the drinking one night and took her for a ride that ended her life." Tears began to streak down Kirk's face. "Don't do it anymore. Damn it . . . you have to stop making bad decisions, Kevin."

"I hear ya," said Kevin, forcing the words through the lump in his throat.

CHAPTER 61

Kirk walked into the church once again. *I guess I'm having another vision,* he thought to himself, remembering he had made it to his apartment in Mankata.

The church was dark and quiet. The only sound was Kirk's footsteps. The last time the church was this dark in his dreams was when he was a child with the dragon. Suddenly Kirk heard a thump from the confessional in the rear of the church.

Kirk's heart skipped a beat. *Oh, no. Not again.*

Kirk was afraid but knew he should open the door. *There has to be a reason I'm here.*

Besides, it's just a dream, thought Kirk, trying to reassure himself.

Kirk's heart was racing as he reached for the doorknob. He slowly turned it and began to open the door. Suddenly two red eyes appeared inside the confessional. "YOU!" said a loud voice inside the small room.

Kirk fell backwards onto the ground.

"YOU . . . still believe in dragons at your age," said Joe, laughing as he came out of the confessional.

"Why did you do that?" asked Kirk still dumbfounded.

"Just for a little humor. Give yourself a couple of seconds, and it will make you smile too."

Joe was right. Kirk began to smile as Joe helped him off the floor.

"Let's have a seat, Kirk," said Joe, motioning towards the front of the church.

The pair walked slowly to the front pew and sat down.

"You did a wonderful job, Kirk," said Joe in a low voice that toned down the playful mood they felt just a minute before.

"It felt good, Joe. It felt good to look past my needs, past anything that affects my life and worry more about someone else's. I forgot. For the past three days, I forgot the guilt. I haven't felt it, and that is something I haven't done for too long. I feel good about myself for putting someone else's troubles in front of my own."

"I have someone here who would like to talk to you, Kirk," said Joe.

Kirk's mind raced as he thought of who might want to see him. The back door of the church opened, and a man dressed in robes with a hood over his head walked in.

"Is that . . ." Kirk could not finish the question.

"Yes," replied Joe. "That is Jesus."

Kirk stepped into the aisle and fell to his knees. He shook at the thought of who he was about to see. His body tingled.

"Kirk. Look at me, Kirk."

Kirk forced himself to look at Jesus. He had never felt so humbled in his life as to be standing in the presence of Christ.

The area around Jesus seemed to be lit up from his presence alone. The darkness that had filled the church was gone and was now suffused with light.

Kirk looked into his face. His face was the same as it appeared on all the statues and pictures he had seen, but something in his face brought a peace Kirk had never felt before. It was similar to the peace he saw in Larry Kincaid's eyes in Indemnity, only so much stronger.

"You have questions you would like to ask me," said Jesus. "Sit with me."

Kirk took a seat in the pew, and Jesus sat next to him. Kirk had imagined many times in his life what he would say if given this opportunity, but the awe of the moment seemed to take away his ability to speak.

"I'll speak first to help you," said Jesus with a smile. "Some of your questions will not be answered, but it's good for you to ask and keep searching for the answer."

There was a pause as he waited for Kirk to begin.

"For the past five years I've fantasized about what Sarah would say to me. Would she tell me she forgives me for ending her life? Or would she say nothing and walk away? I've imagined she would forgive me, but I suppose that is what my mind wants to hear from her." Kirk took a deep breath before continuing. "I learned I can't put those words in hers or anyone else's mouth. Hers and everyone else's decision to forgive me must be their own, and I won't find out in this lifetime if she forgives me." Kirk paused, excited at the possibility. "Will I?"

Jesus smiled. "No. It was not set up to work that way."

"I've been reading the Bible a little more these days," continued Kirk. "In the Gospels it says you came for the sinners. I don't understand why. Why would you come for someone like me who messed up so badly? What about the people who are devout to you their whole life?"

Jesus smiled. "Have you ever saw a parent discipline a child for running out in a busy street because they do not want them to be hit by cars?"

Kirk gave a slight nod.

"Now if that parent has two children and one of them is hit by a car, they're going to take the hurt child to the hospital and take care of him. The loving parents will not forget the other child or his needs, but for a time the hurt child will need extra attention to heal his wounds."

Kirk thought about the connection between himself and the hurt child.

Jesus continued. "Now, after the child has healed, he knows what the parents know about playing in the street and how bad it can hurt. The only reason the other child doesn't play in the street is because his parents told him not to. Sometimes the second child, being innocent and rarely disobedient to the parents, may feel the first child deserved the hurt he felt because he was disobedient. If another child was around who had also been hit by a car, that child who had been healed would feel sympathetic towards the child who had been hit because he knows how easy it is to make a mistake. It's the same way with people and sins. You, Kirk Murphy, know all it takes is one missed step and you get hurt. What do you suppose the healed child will do if he sees a child playing in the street?"

Kirk smiled. "He would tell him to stay out of the street before he gets hurt."

Jesus looked at Kirk. "You've learned so much through your struggle with your guilt. You want others to forgive you, but you need to forgive yourself. I forgive you, Kirk. As soon as you were remorseful, I forgave you, and no matter how hard your life is I will always be with you."

"Will you see Sarah?" asked Kirk.

"Yes."

"Can you tell her," Kirk swallowed, "can you tell her I love her and I'm sorry?"

"She already knows."

The brightest light Kirk had ever seen filled the church. As the light dimmed, Jesus was gone.

"I forgive myself," whispered Kirk.

CHAPTER 62

Kirk turned off the highway onto the gravel road. It had been three years since he had made this trip home. His car was loaded with everything he had decided to keep from Washington.

Kirk pulled into the driveway at his mom's house.

Looks almost the same as the last time I was here, thought Kirk, noticing John had replaced about five hundred feet of the fence that ran from the house to the barn.

"It's about time you made it back," said Kirk's mom, stepping out of the house with John close behind.

"Hey, Mom," said Kirk as she gave him a hug that almost cut off his air supply.

Kirk and his brother shook hands.

"Hey, Kirk, how ya been?"

"Good. Really good. How about you?"

"Busy. I just bought the Milford farm and all their stock. Gave me almost eighty more head of cattle. I'm going to have to hire a hand to help take care of everything. I've been putting in about twelve hours a day and need to put in about five more to keep up."

"I would be interested in that position," said Kirk as the thought of working back on the farm sounded pretty good.

"It doesn't pay much," said John.

"That's okay," said Kirk with a smile. "I don't have a very good résumé."

"Let's go in, and I'll cook you boys something to eat."

Kirk always thought it was funny the way his mom answered every situation with wanting to cook something for them, but he was hungry and hadn't had a good home-cooked meal for some time.

"I'll take you up on that offer, Mom," said Kirk, walking with his arm around her into the house.

CHAPTER 63

Kirk had not stepped into this church for almost six years. He had been here in his visions but had not been physically here for some time. A few things had changed, but Kirk was almost certain his visions showed the church the way he had remembered it.

Kirk sat down in a pew about halfway towards the front. *My whole life seems to have revolved around this church,* thought Kirk as he remembered his childhood dream and the visions he recently had.

"Kirk?" asked a deep voice. Kirk turned to find himself facing Mr. Horton.

"I thought that was you," said Mr. Horton before Kirk could respond. Kirk's heart skipped a beat at the uncertainty he was feeling at facing this man he had hurt so terribly. The last time he had spoken to him he made it clear he did not wish to ever see or talk to him again.

"Can I sit down?" asked Mr. Horton in a tone that calmed Kirk's uneasiness.

"Sure," replied Kirk, scooting over to allow room for him.

After a few seconds that felt like an eternity, Mr. Horton began to speak. "I hated you, Kirk. More than I've ever hated anyone else."

Kirk could not reply because of the knot swelling up in his throat.

Mr. Horton's voice cracked as he continued. "All my adult life I've been a businessman, a good businessman. I've made lots of money over the years. Right now, I would trade all that money for a few minutes with my daughter." He paused to clear his throat before continuing. "You did something one time without considering the consequences of your actions, and it took her life."

Mr. Horton began sobbing as he tried to finish what he was trying to say. Tears ran down Kirk's face. He had never seen Mr. Horton look so broken.

"I've got a letter I want you to read. I've never shown it to anyone else," said Mr. Horton, barely able to get the words out.

Kirk took the letter from him carefully. The envelope looked as though it had been carried around in Mr. Horton's pocket for some time. Mr. Horton turned away from Kirk as he began to read the letter to himself.

Dad,

I was looking forward to going to the concert with you last night. I hope what you had to do at work was more important than how I feel because I was hurt. I shouldn't have expected anything less since that is how it has been my whole life. Kirk wanted to take me out the night of my birthday, but I told him he had to wait until Friday because you were taking me to the concert on Thursday. I spent my seventeenth birthday alone, but tonight Kirk is taking me out, and I can depend on him to do that because he said he would. He may not have a lot of money like you do, but he has something you never have for me. Time.

Mr. Horton gave Kirk a second to digest what he read before continuing. "She left that for me the night she died. It was her last words to me. I was angry at you for taking her life, but I took her life also. A little piece at a time. The ball games I missed, the holidays I wasn't home. I made the decision more than once to take a little piece of her life away from her because I had my business to take care of. My worthless business," he said as though he never resented anything more than the business he had built. "The more I thought about her life being taken from her, the more I realized I was guilty of taking it, depriving her of things she needed to live a fulfilled life, and if I hated someone for taking life from her I had to hate myself."

Mr. Horton grabbed Kirk's shoulder. Kirk looked at him. Both men had tears streaming down their face.

"You gave her life, Kirk. I wouldn't admit to it back then, but you made her happy. She was missing something important, and you filled that space I had left empty by not being there. I forgive you, Kirk, so I can move on with life and because you made her happy when I did not."

The words were hard to understand through the sobbing, but Kirk clearly heard "I forgive you." He had become reluctantly content with the fact he would never hear these words from Mr. Horton.

Kirk was surprised as Mr. Horton wrapped his arms around him. A wave of emotion overtook Kirk as the words sunk in.

"Thank you," sobbed Kirk. "Thank you."

CHAPTER 64

Mr. Horton stood in the small room under the stairway of the home where he was raised in rural Kentucky. The room was tiny for him now. He remembered as a child spending hours in this room. It was his refuge from a father that was usually drunk and always in a bad mood. Mr. Horton would spend hours under this stairway hiding from his dad. His mom knew where he was but would leave him there until his dad passed out for the evening.

"Hello, Kenny."

Mr. Horton did not seem surprised by the old man who appeared behind him.

"You were right, Joe," replied Mr. Horton. "I do feel better now that I've forgiven him and myself. I realize it's time to let Sarah go. She's starting to seem like a good dream I had now, instead of someone I shared part of my life with."

"It is time to move on with your life, Kenny," replied Joe. "God never intended for anyone to live with guilt or to let it take away from the life he intended for you."

"What am I supposed to do now?" asked Mr. Horton.

"What was the mistake you made with Sarah?" Joe asked, letting Mr. Horton answer his own question.

"I didn't spend enough time with her. I spent my whole childhood hiding from my father and swore to myself I would not be like him. I kept that promise because my child never hid from me. She didn't have to. I was never there. I gave her life but didn't share that life with her or teach her how to not take it for granted. But despite my failure to teach her how to love life, she learned. From someone else, she learned good things. She was full of good things I should have enjoyed while she was here."

Joe smiled. "Now go and enjoy the other people in your life that are still with you."

Joe disappeared, leaving Mr. Horton to his thoughts in the little room beneath the stairs until he would wake from this dream.

CHAPTER 65

Kirk took a handkerchief out of his pocket and wiped the sweat from his brow. He was painting the old barn that had been neglected for a few years. A red pickup pulling a cargo trailer pulled into the driveway. Kirk sat his paintbrush down and walked down the hill to greet them.

Kirk saw a man get out of the driver's side and walk around the truck. From the back of the pickup, the man pulled out a wheelchair. Kirk's heart almost jumped out of his chest as he saw Linda step out of the truck and sit down.

"Hello, Kirk," she said with a smile that showed she was delighted to see him.

"Hi, Linda," said Kirk, unable to conceal his mixed emotions of confusion and delight.

"Kirk, I would like for you to meet my father. Dad, this is Kirk."

"Doug," said the man, taking the liberty to introduce himself as more than "Dad." "Pleasure to meet you, Kirk. Linda had some nice things to say about you."

"Dad," said Linda, sounding a little shy about Kirk knowing she spoke well of him.

"Glad to know I make good first impressions," said Kirk, sharing a look with Linda. "What brings you to Lansing?"

"You said one of your goals was to obtain your license for a hot air balloon, but you weren't too sure about it because you've never flown in one. I thought since I was certified to fly one and my dad owned one that I would take you for your test flight to see if you enjoyed it."

"You mean you can fly one?" asked Kirk.

"If you decide you like it, Dad and I thought if you could take a month off sometime you could come up to Lake View. Dad here is a certified instructor. He could train you."

"You can do that?"

"I would even waive the fees if you helped out with some stuff I've been meaning to get done around the house."

"I would take you up on that . . . if I can get my boss to let me off for a little while," said Kirk in a raised tone as he noticed John coming up behind him.

"You've worked here three weeks and you already want time off," said John jokingly. "No wonder you had such poor references."

"Well, let's get it set up and ready to go," said Linda, anxious to take Kirk on his first flight.

Doug pulled the truck out into an open spot in a field he thought would be a suitable launch site.

Kirk could tell from the speed that Doug set the balloon up he had done this many times. Kirk realized quickly the best way he could help was to stay out of Doug's way until he asked for something.

He's not afraid to ask either, thought Kirk to himself as Doug barked orders when he needed an extra hand. *Must be ex-military,* Kirk decided.

*   *   *

"Ready for take-off, Linda?"

"You bet, Dad."

"I'll be on chase. You want to come with me, John?" Doug asked.

"It'll get me out of painting the barn for a couple hours."

Kirk hopped into the basket.

"You have to help me in," said Linda as her father picked her up out of her wheelchair.

Kirk took Linda from her father's arms. He had not held a woman this close for a long time. The smell of her perfume and the touch of her hand draped over his shoulder caused his heart to skip.

As he sat her down in a seat which appeared to be specially made to allow her access to the controls, their eyes met. His mind was telling him to look away, but he couldn't make himself.

"Uhh. What now?" he said, finally breaking the silence.

Linda seemed at a loss for words as she reached up and pulled the handle to allow more fire to heat the balloon. Her father untied the ropes that held the balloon.

Kirk's heart began to beat faster as a sensation similar to going up in an elevator came over him.

"It's better than I imagined," said Kirk, looking down on the farm. He could see all the way into town and all the neighboring houses he had been so familiar with as a child. Everything looked so different from this height, and the ride was so quiet.

"Your troubles won't touch you up here," said Linda who had remained quiet to let Kirk enjoy the experience. "Do you think you might want to come up for a month and learn how to fly one of these?" asked Linda, hoping the answer was yes.

"Linda," said Kirk in a serious tone, "even if I didn't like flying in this today, and I do, I would say I did just so I could go to North Dakota for a month and get to know you a little better."

Kirk knelt down and held Linda's hand so he would be eye level with her. "Since that night in Indemnity, I've thought about you. I know we haven't known each other very long, but something seems to click between us. I know I'm saying a lot here but given the distance between us I don't want to waste time. I hope I didn't just make a fool of myself," he said, looking at her for what he hoped would be a positive response.

From the look on Linda's face it was clear she felt the same way. The wind was gently blowing her hair, and the blue sky matched the color of her eyes perfectly.

She looks so beautiful.

"I was hoping you felt that way," said Linda, brushing her hair back. "Or I would have made a fool out of myself coming from Lake View to give you a ride in this balloon."

"That was a nice gesture. Thank you," said Kirk in a softer tone, leaning towards Linda.

Linda leaned forward to give Kirk a warm, welcomed kiss as they drifted effortlessly over the beautiful countryside, too high above the ground for their troubles to reach them.

EPILOGUE

(Five years later)

Kirk pulled up to the construction crew that the Order had placed a couple miles outside of Indemnity on Highway J. He flashed the lights of his van three times in rapid succession, and a fourth time ten seconds after. The crew pulled the road closed signs out of the way and waved him through.

"This is so cool," said Linda with a smile. "I'm so glad to be with you back in South Dakota on your fifth anniversary of your first time here."

"...and your tenth anniversary," Kirk added. "So much has happened since then." He smiled and grabbed her hand, rubbing the engagement ring. "I never dreamed that my guilt would be so far behind me with nothing but a blessed life to look forward to."

"Me too," returned Linda, bringing his hand to her face and giving it a gentle kiss. "I love you so much."

"I love you too, Linda."

Kirk turned down Highview Road.

"This town hasn't changed," said Kirk as he pulled into a parking spot on the side of the road.

"Probably part of the reason the Order uses it," commented Linda.

"It looks like the festival has already started," Kirk pointed out, noticing that a lot of the carnival rides were already operating.

"Let's stop looking at it and get me in my wheelchair," said Linda in a sarcastic tone. "We've got a couple of anniversaries to celebrate."

"On it," replied Kirk.

Kirk grabbed the wheelchair from the back of the van and brought it to the passenger side. He opened the door and wrapped his arms around Linda and lifted her down into the chair.

"You know I can use the lift in the back and get down myself."

"I know," smiled Kirk, "but I would miss the closeness if I didn't get to help you out. Besides, I'm kind of feeling romantic since this is where we first met," Kirk said with a smile.

Linda smiled back.

"Are you two done with the romantic talk? I'm hoping you have time to say hi to an old friend."

Kirk turned. "Oh wow…Ron…Ron, how have you been?" asked Kirk as he instinctively reached out for a hug at the excitement of seeing Ron after all these years.

He hesitated for a second, not sure he and Ron were on hugging terms.

"AHH…bring it in here, Kirk. I'm glad to see you too. Just a man-hug, though," laughed Ron.

"Let's walk through the carnival, and you two can catch up as we go," interrupted Linda.

"All right," replied Kirk, grabbing the back of her wheelchair and pushing her towards the lights.

"Wow, it is so good to see you, Ron. How's life?"

"Kirk, my heart is full. I succeeded in my mission. Kept him from making my mistake. But I have to tell you, that thing with the devil before I got there…about did me in. Would never have done it without God."

"Same here. The devil was in a church I went to. Unreal some of the things I saw. It made my faith so strong. If God can get me through that, I know there's nothing he won't get me through. I've heard God won't give you more than you can handle, but that was the limit. I'm afraid more may have been too much."

Ron nodded soberly, looking off into the distance.

"Linda here is my hero," continued Kirk. "She did what we did against the devil, but she did it in a wheelchair."

"Kirk, I've told you it wasn't about physical abilities. It was about faith. God had me. I knew it at the end of my trial that I could do it."

"I think sometimes we see people with physical disabilities as weaker...God knows they are stronger," Kirk commented.

"Look at this place," interrupted Ron. "It's so much better to be here for our five-year anniversary than it was to be here the first time. We had lost faith and direction. So good to be here with a focus on God and family."

"Family?" quizzed Kirk.

"Yes," beamed Ron, "we worked it out. Nancy, Nick, Andrew, and me. We're all back together, living under the same roof. Well, Nick left for college last year, and Andrew is leaving for college at the end of this year...two years early. Man, he's a smart kid. They bumped him up. Way ahead of anyone else in his class. It was good to be involved in the last few years. I watched them turn from kids into young men. I helped them make that transition. Something that wouldn't have happened without God and the Order."

"Hey...hey! Everyone up by the steps of the cellar...they want to talk to us...everyone to the cellar steps!" shouted a middle-aged man as he ran by.

"EVERYONE TO THE CELLAR STEPS," more people joined in the announcement.

The crowd's pace quickened as they all moved to the location of the cellar.

"What do you suppose is happening?" asked Linda in a concerned tone.

"Not sure," Kirk responded as he pushed her down the street.

The crowd gathered around the opening of the cellar. Several minutes passed.

"Well, they got us all here," commented Ron.

"There must be three hundred people," estimated Kirk.

The crowd mumbled as they waited to see why they had been pulled from the festival.

Finally, the cellar door opened. Larry Kincaid walked out carrying a microphone.

"Ladies and gentlemen." The voice came from speakers that had been previously placed to the left and right of Larry. "I apologize to interrupt the anniversary of your redemption, but the Order is in need of several of you at this time. At some point the Order will ask all of you to give back. I know you all have settled into your lives and are probably content with your current situation, but the Order is asking you to give back…as it gave to you. It will not be easy, but if your name is called please stay and hear us out. The rest of you can go back to the festival. I fear the battle against evil will tip in their favor if you choose not to join us."

The crowd grew quiet as Larry pulled a folded piece of paper from his shirt pocket.

"Jerry Henderson, Linda Manchester…" Kirk squeezed Linda's shoulder. She reached up and grabbed his hand. Larry continued, "Bill Baxton, Sherry Miller, Kirk Murphy…" Linda squeezed his hand tighter. "John Gifford and Betty Crawford. The rest of you may leave."

Kirk and Ron exchanged a knowing glance.

"I guess I'm done here," stated Ron.

"I guess so," responded Kirk slowly. "Man, it was good to see you."

"You too, Kirk," said Ron. "Good luck with whatever the Order needs from you."

"Thanks, Ron." The two men exchanged a handshake.

Ron walked away.

"What do you think they need from us?" Linda asked.

"I'm not sure," replied Kirk, "but whatever it is, count me in."